- **THE MYSTERIOUS WU FANG:
THE CASE OF THE GREEN DEATH**

THE MYSTERIOUS WU FANG™

THE CASE OF THE GREEN DEATH

By Robert J. Hogan

ALTUS PRESS • 2017

CHAPTER 1
THE FACE IN THE FOG

A S THOUGH a curtain had been drawn quickly away, a rift appeared in the sodden fog that shrouded London's Chinatown. In that break two men might have been seen standing well back in the shadow of a narrow doorway. The fog closed in again like a veil of mystery.

The ghostly air was suddenly split with the distant sound of a deep-throated gong. One of the two men tensed. Instinctively, he moved closer to the other.

"What was that?" he whispered hoarsely.

This was Jerry Hazard, special international correspondent of the McNulty News Syndicate. The muscles of his square-jawed face contracted and relaxed.

In striking contrast, Val Kildare, former No. 1 government man, now working on his own in pursuit of the most dangerous man in the world, remained calm. Kildare was slightly taller than Hazard, lean and muscular.

His keen eyes shifted quickly and focused on Hazard's face in the dark mist. Hazard could see a smile play across his friend's thin lips.

"Probably the Chinese are being called to prayer in one of their underground temples," Kildare ventured.

Hazard couldn't take it so lightly.

"It might be a special meeting of the Chang Li," he argued.

Something sputtered from the machine
that the black cloth shrouded.

"Perhaps," Kildare admitted. "We may find out if we stay here long enough."

Hazard shifted uneasily.

"It's getting on my nerves," he confessed. "Here we've been standing hour after hour, watching. And for what? You aren't even sure that Wu Fang is here in London's Limehouse."

"No?" Kildare smiled. "How about the article that you wrote

yourself concerning the new weapon of war that an inventor is working on here in England?"

"Yes," Hazard argued, "but there's nothing definite about it."

"Nothing definite," Kildare smilingly admitted, "except the fact that the news leaked out concerning the inventor's first trial of a machine that kills effectively at short range."

"Yes," Hazard frowned, "but the type of machine or apparatus—there was nothing definite about that. Nobody knows anything about it except the inventor himself."

Kildare gave a short nod.

"Right," he said. "But you may depend upon it that Wu Fang will know just as soon as it's superhumanly possible. And when that yellow devil does learn the secret, all the peoples on the earth except the Orientals will be in danger. Then we'll all be obliged to dance at his bidding, and life, particularly for the white race, wouldn't be worth living. Moreover, since this article of yours came out in America, there has been no trace whatever of any activity by Wu Fang in New York's Chinatown. Wong Chu himself, one of the most powerful members of the Chang Li, admitted that Wu Fang was gone, although he didn't know where."

Hazard stiffened as the fog-laden air was again filled with the deep-throated bong of the Chinese bell.

"There it goes again," he hissed.

Kildare shook his head.

"I'm not nearly as interested in the sound of that gong, Jerry," he said, "as I am in learning who the inventor of this death machine is and in reaching him."

"Then let's get out of this place," Hazard suggested. "You certainly won't find him down here."

"No," Kildare admitted, "perhaps not. But the Chinese undercover man of Scotland Yard has discovered one thing for us, due to my wireless message while we were crossing from New York. He has learned that a party of Chinamen, who tally very nicely with the description of Wu Fang and his agents, have taken up quarters somewhere in the block on the opposite side of the street from where we're standing now."

Hazard stared into the thick, blinding mist that enveloped London's Chinatown.

"Maybe," he ventured, "we could see something if this confounded fog would lift."

Again Kildare smiled.

"Wu Fang is playing in his usual run of luck," he commented. "Even the gods seem to favor that yellow devil. But I think we're getting him cornered this time. And by heaven, we're going to trail him until we finish him, so that civilization will be safe."

The fog lifted for a moment so that they could see across the street, where the squalid fronts of the buildings, except for the very narrow sidewalk, came down virtually to the gutter itself.

Hazard stared across for a moment until the fog closed in again. He shifted his eyes quickly to the government man's face, saw a keen light of anticipation there.

"Look here, Kildare," he said huskily. "You're watching for someone. You're expecting something definite to happen. What is it?"

He felt Kildare's eyes upon him for an instant. Then the government man was speaking.

"Yes," he admitted, "I am. My brain has been pretty full of this case since we landed. I guess I've neglected to let you in on some things that have come up. I learned from Scotland Yard that Bertrand Trask has loaned a huge sum of money to the inventor of this deadly mechanism."

Hazard's eyes widened in surprise.

"YOU MEAN," he demanded, "Bertrand Trask, the biggest banker in London?"

"Exactly," Kildare said, nodding.

"But how," Hazard argued, "would Scotland Yard be able to learn that Trask had loaned money to the inventor and still not be able to find out his name?"

"That," said Kildare, "as you should know, since you wrote up the story for the news syndicate, is the way that the information leaked out in the first place. You got the story from Scotland Yard. They, in turn, had learned from Trask that he had loaned money to finance the development of this invention.

"Trask is a very powerful man in England. So powerful, in fact, that Scotland Yard didn't dare press him too far for questioning. He admitted that he was financing this invention, but refused to disclose the name of the inventor. He explained that it would expose the inventor to international intrigue.

"He and his only son, Gerald, are in complete control of their banking institution. For a rich man's son, Gerald Trask hasn't done so badly, following in his father's footsteps. But he probably would be lost if his father died. He hasn't got the shrewd business instinct of the old man. Another thing I have learned, is that Trask is as tight-fisted as they come. That's the way he has built up his enormous banking business. He never loans out a dollar without getting ample security for it."

"But what's that got to do with our standing here and watching for something to happen?" Hazard demanded.

"We are standing here," Kildare went on, "because I'm expecting someone. I've got this entire block surrounded by Scotland Yard men. Confound it, if this accursed fog would only lift!"

Suddenly, Kildare was gripping Hazard's wrist and pressing so tightly that the newspaperman winced. Now Hazard knew why the government man had done that. He could hear a soft *pad, pad, pad* of feet coming up the sidewalk, very close to the building that sheltered them.

A form, shadowy and vague, loomed out of the fog for an instant. It was within easy reach, scarcely more than two feet away.

Kildare and Hazard both remained rigid, moving not a single muscle. They saw the face in the fog. It was dark and yellow with sunken cheeks—the face of a half-starved coolie.

Then, as though a magician had waved his wand over the Oriental's head, the yellow man vanished before their eyes, even as Kildare shot out an arm to catch him.

"Who was it?" Hazard gasped.

"Someone," Kildare said, "who knows we're here. I haven't the least doubt of it. And it won't be long before we hear more from him."

"Good Lord!" Hazard breathed. "I never saw anyone move so fast in my life. Did you see which way he went?"

"No," Kildare said. "God, what fog!"

Now the government man raised his voice to a monotone that could be heard almost all the way across the street. With a little laugh, he said, "I'll bet that coolie was scared to death when he saw us lurking here in the doorway. Likely he won't sleep for a week."

Hazard looked at his friend in amazement. They had been standing in this doorway, speaking in low, guarded whispers. Why was Kildare talking now in such a loud tone? Had he suddenly gone mad? As those thoughts rushed through his brain, Hazard suddenly felt Kildare's lips close to his ear.

"And now," the government man was saying in a whisper, barely audible even to Hazard, "can you walk without making the slightest sound?"

Hazard nodded.

"All right," Kildare whispered. "But remember, our lives depend upon absolute silence."

On tiptoe, Kildare led Hazard out of the doorway to the sidewalk. They kept close to the building fronts as they proceeded carefully, step after step.

Hazard didn't know why, but he was sure from what Kildare had said that even the squeak of a shoe would seal their doom. They moved on at a maddeningly slow gait, feeling first with their toes on the sidewalk, then putting their weight on the balls of their feet, balancing, and feeling ahead with their other foot for the next step. The suspense was appalling, intensified by the density of the fog.

It seemed to Hazard, as they moved, that objects appeared and vanished beside them, in front of them, behind them, hidden in the fog. Beings that had eyes that pierced the fog as theirs could not.

They must have gone thirty feet up the street when Kildare stopped in a narrow doorway that reeked with the stench of the Orient.

Again, Kildare's lips were very close to the newspaperman's ear. "I think we made it OK, but I'm not sure," he whispered.

"What is it? What do you expect?" Hazard hissed.

"Listen!"

That was all Kildare would answer.

Seconds passed like dragging hours. Hazard's ears were tuned to catch the slightest sound that might come from any source. He was wondering frantically what Kildare might mean by this.

There was an awful suspense about it all. If they were heard in their movement away from that doorway, they would be finished. What did Kildare know that he didn't? What did he suspect? He marveled at the government man's intuition.

Kildare was gripping his arm again, pressing tightly for utter silence. Jerry Hazard heard a sound come, ever so softly in the fog-drenched night.

Pad!

Kildare tightened his grip still more. There it was again.

Pad!

The sound was like the soft thud of a foot against one of the paving stones; it seemed to come from the center of the street, opposite the door where they had first been hiding.

KILDARE WAS leaning out of the doorway where they stood now, poking his head out so that he could listen more clearly.

Then another sound, dull, low and ominous.

Thump!

Instantly, it reminded Hazard of a rat or a mouse dropping from a shelf to a floor below.

"Wait," Kildare snapped. "There will be another."

Even as he spoke, there was a second thump like the first, coming from the direction of the doorway where they had been before. Then there was the sound of softly running feet, dying away after a few steps in the darkness.

They waited, motionless. After a lapse of several minutes, Kildare spoke. "There. I think the danger is over."

Jerry Hazard shook his head in a baffled sort of way. He was completely in a fog, mentally as well as physically.

"I've never doubted your knowing what you were talking about, Kildare," he said. "I don't now, but you have certainly got me stumped. What was the danger? What made you suspect it? And what makes you think it's over now?"

Kildare was smiling tolerantly.

"It's quite simple, Jerry," he said. "You would have thought of it yourself—if it had come to you. I assumed that the Chinaman who passed close by our hiding place and saw us was an agent of Wu Fang. Can't you imagine from that what I suspected?"

"Good Heavens? You mean the death beasts?"

"Exactly," Kildare nodded. "That's why we left as silently as we did, so that this agent wouldn't know that we had left that spot. He probably knows every street in Limehouse like a book. He was gone just long enough to get two of Wu Fang's deadly beasts and return. He held them so they couldn't bite him, and when he was in the middle of the street directly opposite where we were hiding, he simply tossed them into the doorway. We weren't there, of course, so—"

In the cramped doorway, Hazard felt Kildare's broad, lean shoulders shrug.

"But you say that the danger is past," the newspaperman protested. "How can you say that when you know those beasts are running about?"

"They may be running about," Kildare chuckled softly, "but I'll wager they're not very comfortable."

"Comfortable?" Hazard gasped.

"Yes, Jerry," the government man said. "You see, when even a tiny animal or bug takes arsenic into its stomach, it doesn't make it feel particularly at ease."

"Arsenic?" Hazard repeated. "You mean—"

Kildare was nodding slowly.

"Yes," he said. "I've been carrying a little supply of a special poison rat biscuit that I concocted myself. I think it's very attractive to them, if my guess at what the little death beasts like

The government man was falling over the dead body in the gutter.

is correct. I dropped a couple of them before we left that doorway."

Instinctively, Hazard started toward the sidewalk, but Kildare drew him back.

"There isn't time to look now," he said. "Besides, it would be too dangerous to let the agent know that we're still moving about."

Obediently, Hazard crowded back into the doorway. He shook his head in wonder. Suddenly, the newspaperman felt Kildare grow tense as he listened intently.

"There comes something now," he said. Already, Hazard's ears had caught the sound of a motor coming nearer and nearer. The fog lifted for an instant, then settled again.

Hazard heard Kildare mumble under his breath, "If we would only get a break and this fog would lift."

From somewhere out of that ghostly white mist the rumble of a car grew louder. Hazard's hand slipped into his gun pocket.

Kildare must have divined his intention from the movement, for he said in a low whisper, "Never mind that, Jerry. If there's any shooting to be done, I'll tell you when. This is someone whom we want to keep from getting hurt."

Hazard's brain was spinning. How did Kildare know whom to expect?

A clock in a far-off church tower was striking twelve times.

Hazard felt Kildare move out of the doorway just a little, heard him say to himself, "That's right. An appointment at midnight. We're in luck, if this fog would only—"

There was a low squeal as brakes were applied. The car was drawing up to the curb across the street.

Kildare stepped softly out on the sidewalk and was almost lost to Hazard in the mist. The newspaperman stepped quickly beside him.

He heard a door latch snap. Someone was getting out of the car over there, not thirty feet away. Someone whom they couldn't see through the fog.

Kildare stopped short as a breeze swept up the dark, winding street of Limehouse and rent a hole in the fog through which they could see temporarily.

A taxi was outlined clearly against the dark buildings. The driver was leaning out the window as the passenger paid him. They could see the passenger's face very faintly in the light of the dash bulb as it reflected on his countenance.

Hazard gasped. The passenger was Gerald Trask. But what would the great banker's son and partner be doing at midnight in London's Limehouse?

Now Kildare was dashing across the street, shouting, "Trask! Trask! Stop!"

But the taxi was parked against the curb between them and young Trask. In order to catch him, they would have to run around either end of the car.

Suddenly, a shrill cry of terror cut the fog.

CHAPTER 2
THE CRIME BEAST STRIKES

KILDARE WAS dashing around the rear of the car. Hazard tried to get around the front, but the car started up suddenly and almost ran him down. He darted back toward the rear of the car and around it as the taxi roared away.

He seemed completely alone in that awful tangle of mist, but he knew that Kildare couldn't be far away.

In the darkness, Hazard collided with a bang against the doors of a little shop. Kildare wasn't there.

He whirled and darted out on the sidewalk again, fumbling along the front of the building, calling in a low tone, "Kildare! Kildare!"

He heard a soft padding of footsteps and next Kildare's voice calling, "Did you follow him? Did you see where he went?"

"No," Hazard hissed. "You were ahead. I tried to get around the front of the cab but the driver pulled out. He must have been scared."

For a moment, Kildare stood erect, motionless, trying to pierce the fog with his keen eyes.

Then he said in a hoarse whisper, "Young Trask passed through a doorway that we can't break down. If we can find that door, we'll have the place. Come on."

With that, Kildare darted around the end of the short, low railing that Hazard had stumbled against. They were going down a flight of steep steps that led to the basement below.

Hazard heard a hollow sound through the pitch blackness.

15

"Kildare, are you all right?" he asked.

"Yes," came the reply. "That was my shoulder smacking the door. I think it's made of oak planking, but it's as strong as iron."

The government man's voice was low and tense as he gripped Hazard's shoulders.

"Around this way with your back against mine," he said.

Hazard turned.

"That's it. Now my left shoulder against the door and your right one. Come on. We've got to break it down."

Hazard could feel the government man's back against his. Muscles strained desperately.

They braced their feet against the narrow steps and pushed with all their might, but it was as though they were pressing against a stone wall. The heavy but narrow door didn't bulge, didn't even groan under the strain.

"Back now," Kildare whispered. "Let's get a start and crash the door at the same time."

They stepped back a pace, which was as far as they could move in the little space at the bottom of the stairs.

Softly Kildare counted, "One, two, three!"

Bam!

Their bodies shot forward together, collided with a heavy thud against the door.

"Wait a minute," Kildare said, and fumbled about in the darkness.

"It's no use," he decided. "We can't crash it this way. Not the two of us."

Now Hazard felt over the door. It was heavy, windowless, as solid as though it were a concrete wall.

"That's funny," he said. "I looked over this street pretty thoroughly with you in the daylight, but I don't remember any door like this at the bottom of these stairs."

"No," Kildare said, "I'll show you."

He took Hazard's hands and moved them over to the left side of the little space at the bottom of the stairs.

"Feel that?" he asked.

Hazard felt his hands come in contact with an even depression at the side.

"Clever, that," Kildare said. "Look here. This entrance has a double door. I remember the place distinctly. It's a Chinese laundry, but that's only a front for some sort of devilish business. This is an emergency door that's closed now. It opens outward. In order to break in we've got to pretty nearly push in the whole side of the building.

"In the daytime, when someone is apt to be looking about, this door is swung back into the recess. I'll gamble the inside of it is finished so that it matches exactly the passageway down the stairs."

"I can't see," Hazard argued, "what makes you so certain that this is the door that young Trask entered. What is he doing here in this place? Certainly the son of the biggest banker in London shouldn't be—"

"If you think," Kildare interrupted, "that Gerald Trask came here because he's lined up with Wu Fang, you're wrong. Trask came of his own free will. He was scared to death or he wouldn't have run when I called his name. He felt for some reason that he must come here.

"I know he's behind this door because I've examined every other entrance. We could break down any of them but not this one."

"Then why not crash in one of the others and try to find a passage that will lead below into here?" Hazard ventured.

"That wouldn't do us any good," Kildare snapped. "Wu Fang isn't that simple. He chose this place because it's the only means of entrance into some hideout of his or his agents. Perhaps you didn't see what I saw when I got around the end of the cab. Gerald Trask wasn't alone after he left the cab."

"What?" Hazard demanded.

"That's right," Kildare confirmed. "I saw two forms against the side of the building. I couldn't make them out very clearly because the fog closed in just at that time. When I saw them, they were lunging at Trask from behind. Trask was lured here on some pretext and unless I'm—"

Suddenly, Kildare turned and started up the stairs again. "THERE ARE six Scotland Yard men surrounding this block," he said. "We've got to get their help."

He pointed down the street to the left.

"You go that way," he said. "You won't find any until you turn the corner. Then look for them on the side of the street opposite this block. They'll be watching in a doorway, if—"

Hazard didn't hear the rest of Kildare's speech, for the government man was already striding off in the opposite direction. The newspaperman broke into a run.

He met no one in the fog as he reached the corner, turned, and crossed the street.

He was moving more slowly now. He had a strange, lonely feeling as he searched those empty doorways for the Scotland Yard man. He passed one after another without finding any living soul there. Even the dark, befogged air itself seemed tinged with menace. But he forced himself to go on.

He reached the next corner. All the doorways so far had been vacant. Fearsome as they had seemed to him, he had entered every one, had made a thorough search of the block.

He turned the next corner. Again he searched doorways, alleys, steep stairways that led off the street. All was deathly still. Nothing moved in that awful fog. Nothing except—

He stopped suddenly to listen. He was sure he had heard a sound behind him. Someone had been following him. Perhaps it was Kildare. He stepped quickly into a doorway and waited. No, it couldn't be Kildare. He didn't come on. Whoever it was, was waiting, too. A chill ran up and down Hazard's spine, as though a clammy hand had been placed there.

Hazard stepped out of the doorway again and hurried on, inspecting the doorways now with a swift plunge of his fist in the darkness.

There was again a single padding sound on the paving. He blinked his eyes as he turned, trying to clear them so that he could see better into the darkness. But he could see nothing except the billows of mist.

He moved on to the next doorway, walking on tiptoe. Nothing there. In the next—

His heart leaped wildly as he stumbled over a form lying across the sidewalk. For a moment, he stood there tense, rigid, ready to strike if something attacked.

He heard a soft step, this time ahead of him. He knew by now that he had gone halfway around the block. This must be Kildare.

He called in a soft whisper. Kildare's voice came back to him, "Yes, Jerry."

"Look here," Hazard whispered. "There's something here, Kildare."

"I was afraid of that," the government man's voice came back.

Then Kildare loomed before him out of the fog. Hazard saw him bending over the form at their feet, saw his fingers going rapidly over the still body.

"It's one of the Scotland Yard men who were watching," Kildare said. "The other one is in the doorway where he fell."

Hazard gasped.

"You mean he got all of them?"

"Yes." Kildare nodded. "You didn't find any in your tour around the block, did you?"

"No," Hazard said. "All the doorways were empty."

"I found the other two on the end street. Four of them gone and two missing."

There was a horrible, awed silence for a minute. Then Hazard put his lips to Kildare's ear.

"I'm being followed," he whispered.

"Yes, naturally," Kildare answered. "So am I. I have an idea that we've been followed ever since we landed in London."

Kildare suddenly grew tense as he spoke again in a hoarse whisper.

"Jerry, if you value your life, run for it."

Jerry Hazard stared at him in astonishment.

"You mean," he hissed, "that you want me to—"

That was as far as he got. Val Kildare made a sudden lunge, arms outstretched. With superhuman force, he struck Hazard in the chest, and the newspaperman was hurled back.

He heard another sound at the same time. He wasn't sure what it was, although he thought he had heard it before.

Kildare had leaped from his crouched position beside the body of the Scotland Yard man and Hazard heard him say softly, "I'm going through with it just as I promised him."

That was all. Then Kildare uttered his name and one word, "Jerry—run!"

He was standing straight, stiff as a ramrod as he said it. Then Hazard saw him totter and pitch forward. He tried to catch him but he couldn't make it in time. The government man was falling to the sidewalk over the body of the dead Englishman.

"Run for your life!" What had Kildare meant by that? Had this master government agent divined something that was coming without seeing it?

Hazard was bending over him, saying, "Kildare! Kildare! What is it? What hit you? Speak to me."

Awful panic seized Hazard. Horrible agents of Wu Fang were trailing him, perhaps surrounding him at this very moment.

His mind flashed like lightning from one thought to another. His beautiful Mohra—was she safe? There was Gerald Trask.

What had happened to him? Why had he come here? What had happened to Kildare? Why had he said, "Run for your life!"

But he couldn't leave Kildare lying here on the ground while he went for help. And still, what had he meant by telling Hazard to leave him? He often gave strange orders, this master detective. Orders that were to be followed out regardless of how ridiculous they might appear.

So Hazard, partly because he was in a panic and partly because Kildare had ordered it, leaped to his feet and started in a wild dash down the street.

HE HAD taken scarcely two steps when he heard a sound that came from just ahead. It was exactly like the one he had heard an instant before Kildare dropped. He recognized it now as the sound of a sarbacan, the unerring blowpipe used by the South American Indians and the *dyacks* of Borneo.

He felt a sudden, numbing sensation in the right side of his neck and the shock of paralysis shot through him.

He struggled desperately to break the fall, but his legs buckled and his arms didn't move. He pitched headlong, sprawling across the curb into the filth of the gutter.

Things grew dim about him. He heard the swift beat of feet, coming to his ears like thunder. For a moment, he heard his heart pounding wildly, sending the echo through his tortured head. Then the fog and the night and unconsciousness closed in about him.

When Hazard was able to open his eyes again, he found himself in a strange underground room. He stared about groggily.

The walls were covered with Oriental drapes and tapestries. Along one side of the room was a row of bunks and beside each one was a little table. Hazard recognized the place instantly. It was an opium den. But there was no evidence now of pipes or trays on the tables containing the usual furnishings for the opium addict. In fact, the four bunks on that side were all empty, except one.

Hazard stared at the figure that lay there. The face was half hidden, but nevertheless, he recognized the features of Gerald Trask, the banker's son. He was bound securely to something behind him that Hazard couldn't see.

Young Trask was fully conscious, his face white and drawn. "Stop them!" he gasped. "Stop them! They'll kill everybody. They have—"

A half-naked giant attendant, brown-skinned and stinking, was leaping across the room. His great open palm flashed through the air in a blur of movement and struck Gerald Trask full in the mouth, knocking his head back with a jerk.

There was no command to be silent, just that loud smacking sound in the face of the young banker.

Hazard was being carried between two stalwart Chinese. His head was clear and consciousness had returned, but as yet, his body was paralyzed, except for his faculties of sight and hearing. He tried to talk, but it was impossible. Just ahead of him, Kildare was being unceremoniously dragged across the floor.

Trask occupied the first bunk. Kildare was being taken toward the third, and Hazard to the second. That left one, the farthest down the line, that was empty.

So far as Hazard could see, the four attendants and the powerful brute who had struck Trask, together with their prisoners, were the only occupants of the room at the moment.

Kildare slumped limply. His eyes were closed; his mouth gaped open. Before they reached the middle bunk where they were taking him, Hazard saw Kildare rolled into the third. The two attendants were binding his hands and legs.

That was all Hazard saw, for at that moment, they tossed him into the middle bunk. Arms went behind him. He couldn't see or feel what was going on, but he could smell the stench of the unwashed bodies of the two men who bound him.

He was facing the outside of the room so that he could see all that took place, although he couldn't see into the bunks occupied by Kildare and Trask. Apparently, they had Kildare securely tied, too, for the Malayans and Chinese filed out, passing behind a drape on the other side of the bunks.

Now that they were alone, Hazard was thinking quite clearly. His immediate concern was for Kildare. He tried to speak, tried to make his throat work, but to no avail.

Desperately, he tested his arms and legs. No use. All sense of feeling was gone from him. And Kildare was still unconscious.

He began to take more particular note of his surroundings. The air was stuffy in the underground space. He could see no doors leading in from the outside. This, he guessed, was the opium den for which the Chinese laundry at the bottom of those steps served as a front.

There was no sound from any quarter as the minutes dragged by. There was only the awful certainty that Kildare had been right. They were in the clutches of Wu Fang, the Dragon Lord of Crime and Emperor of Death. They were as helpless as though they were infants at the mercy of savage wild beasts.

As that thought flashed through Hazard's mind, a gong sounded. It was soft, muted, and deliberate, like the deep-noted gong that might be rung at the entrance of a great ruler's throne room. And as it reached Hazard's ears, he suddenly became aware of a feeling that there was another person in the room.

He shifted his eyes, which were the only part of his body over which he had any control. Wu Fang had come from somewhere, perhaps from behind one of the drapes.

His narrow, gaunt shoulders were slightly bent. The brilliant green eyes in his long, sunken-cheeked face with its enormous forehead were gloating. He clasped his long-nailed, slim-fingered hands before him and his heavy yellow embroidered robe rustled as he walked to a point before the three bunks. His thin lips turned up at the corners in a smile that was horrible. Horrible because it was so fiendishly calm and sure.

And then the yellow devil laughed a soft but high-pitched chuckle. His green, slant eyes shifted from one bunk to another, focused on Kildare.

"IT IS very gratifying to have you all here," Wu Fang said. "I see"—his gaze shifted to Hazard—"that you, Mr. Hazard, are the only one who is fully conscious. That is, perhaps, most unfortunate for you. But have no fear. Your friend, Mr. Kildare, will regain consciousness before very long."

The yellow fiend's smile broadened as he continued. "We are preparing for a little experiment as rapidly as the apparatus can be reconstructed for the purpose. You see"—here he bent his benign smile upon the bunk where Gerald Trask was bound—"Mr. Trask was good enough to bring with him tonight the secret of the new invention which he and his father are financing. When we are ready, we will use you three gentlemen for the experiment. We must have virile types for this test, that we may be sure the apparatus kills quickly, and with the proper amount of pain to the victim. Each of you answers the description 'virile.'"

Wu Fang's shoulders shook as he chuckled to himself.

"So as you lie in your bunks—ah, Mr. Trask, I see you are regaining consciousness again. You will be the first to go before the instrument that is to make me world-powerful. And next, Mr. Hazard, you will undergo the trial. And Mr. Kildare, he will come last. It will be a pleasure for me to have him watch the proceedings as long as possible."

The Dragon Lord of Crime turned and clapped his hands four times. Another man entered the room. He was tall and powerful, obviously an Englishman. He bowed deeply before Wu Fang, and the yellow fiend gave an order.

"You will stay in here," he said, "until I return. You will make sure that my guests do not untie their bindings and escape. You know the consequences if such a thing happens, of course."

The Englishman bowed again.

"Yes, Master," he said meekly.

Wu Fang turned back to Hazard for a parting word.

"You will have a little time left to think," he said, "while I supervise the completion of the murder machine. But I would advise you, Mr. Hazard, not to waste your time thinking of the safety of Mohra, your beautiful one who was once my little flower. I received a cablegram a few minutes ago from my agents in New York, advising me that Mohra is with them, eagerly awaiting my return."

CHAPTER 3
THE MURDER MACHINE

THAT LAST remark drove Jerry Hazard close to insanity. He struggled frantically to get free. But those struggles were mere mental convulsions. The ropes still bound him to the wall. He couldn't feel them cut into his flesh, but he knew they were there.

Wu Fang turned away and left the room. The Englishman whom he had left on guard glanced first at Kildare's bunk, then down at Hazard, who was trying to speak.

The guard nodded with satisfaction as he made sure that Hazard was still helpless. He moved to the end of the bunk where Gerald Trask lay, obviously returning to consciousness. Hazard could hear him trying to say something. Then words came more distinct.

"Listen," he pleaded, "is Wu Fang gone?"

No answer from the guard.

"I tell you you'll never regret letting me and the others out of this," Gerald Trask's voice rasped on. "I'll see that you're paid well for our release. And I'll guarantee protection against Wu Fang if he tries to get revenge against you. I'll—"

The English guard chuckled softly.

"I say now, that's a good one. Protect me from Wu Fang. You do not know him well, or else, I can assure you, you would know that no one is safe from Wu Fang."

Hazard's mad brain was spinning round and round. How well he knew the truth of the statement the guard had uttered. But he only half realized what was going on about him. Mohra! Wu Fang had said that she was in the clutches of his agents in New York's Chinatown. Nothing could be worse.

He tried to relax his brain. Everything was lost. He might as well take his fate—and Mohra's—with the best grace possible. Wu Fang would do exactly as he had threatened. Gradually, Hazard gave up every possible hope of ever seeing the light of day again. Of seeing Mohra. If he only had a fighting chance—

The guard was not one of Wu Fang's demon agents. He wasn't Chinese or Malayan. He was English. And his dress was that of an ordinary businessman. Except for his height, which was about six feet, he wouldn't have stood out particularly in any crowd.

Why was this man placed to guard them when there were so many hideous Orientals to do the guarding?

Hazard found the answer to his wonder in the next minute.

The Englishman, after pacing up and down several times, turned and stood before Trask.

"I say, look here," he ventured in a low voice, "we're both in a bit of the same boat, you know. The Master, Wu Fang, has me where I can't move about a great deal, as I wish. And you are in the same fix, what? So why not"—here his voice dropped so that it was almost inaudible to Hazard—"work together on this? Secretly, of course."

"Work with you?" Trask was heard to whisper.

"Righto," the other went on. "You see, in spite of being tied up to Wu Fang for the very good money which he pays me as one of his agents, I'm still a bit of a lover of the King and country. England should have this invention to use for her own protection, you know. I mean to say, this is going a bit too far, giving up my country, and all that sort of thing."

"You mean you'll help keep the invention away from Wu Fang?" Trask breathed in astonishment. "I say, that's sporting of you. But how?"

"Listen to me closely," the guard whispered. "I've got to go through with this—keeping you here, I mean. I can't change that. But if I knew who the inventor was, and where I could find him working on the vast improvement that he hopes to make in the death apparatus, I could go to him, tonight—when I'm relieved here in an hour. I would go to him and warn him that he must guard his secret most carefully. That he must get out of the country, you know, before Wu Fang kills him and—"

Hazard saw through that. There was something worth fighting for. He saw now that Wu Fang had planted this suave

Englishman, a fellow countryman of Trask's, to get the name of the inventor from him.

He struggled. Worked with all his mental power to move his arms and legs. To speak.

Then suddenly he was speaking in a mumbled jargon.

"Don't tell him," he managed to get out. "Don't tell him. He's tricking you. He's been planted here, Trask, by Wu Fang—to try and work the information out of you that he can't get himself."

"But, I say," Trask ventured. "He may be—"

But the Englishman at that very moment was playing his hand wrong. He leaped across the space that separated him from Hazard. His heavy foot was traveling through the air as he kicked it at Hazard's face.

The toe of the English shoe caught Hazard between the eyes. And as stars appeared before him and darkness closed in, he heard the Englishman's voice crack out:

"I'll teach you to mind your own business."

Everything faded, then, about Hazard. But there was no pain from the kick in the face, as the narcotic still gripped him.

HE HAD no idea how long he had been out. Probably not more than two or three minutes. Trask was insisting that he would never tell the name of the inventor now. The Englishman had shown his true colors when he had attacked Hazard.

The Englishman turned and strode to the far end of the room. There he vanished behind a drape, the same way Wu Fang had gone.

"Trask!" That was Hazard speaking in a low voice.

"Yes."

"This is Jerry Hazard. You didn't tell him?"

"Never," Trask whispered defiantly.

"Good," Hazard said. "Can you get those ropes off your wrists and legs?"

"Heaven knows I've been trying," Trask panted. "I can't budge them. Can you get free?"

"I'm still paralyzed," Hazard mumbled. "Can't move."

He raised his voice a little louder. "Kildare! Kildare!"

No answer. Trask was speaking again.

"Was that you that shouted at me when I got out of the cab?"

"Yes," Hazard told him. "If you had stopped, you might not be in—"

"I know—now," Trask said. "But the whole thing gave me the jitters. My father telephoned me to come down here with the plan of the machine that was in our private safe. He said he was here making special arrangements and he needed the plans. Told me I should say nothing of his call, but come at once."

"And you recognized his voice?" Hazard demanded.

"Yes, that is, I was sure at first. He spoke in a whisper. It sounded like him. I wouldn't swear even now that it wasn't he. I thought all the time he was in Paris on business."

"Do you know that he isn't here?" Hazard asked.

"I—I confess, I'm all at sea," Trask said. "If he is here, then—"

His voice broke off in a choked sob. He continued. "But if he isn't here and you should get out—you have a better chance than I—get to him as soon as possible. Tell him—"

The words ceased. Hazard heard a soft footstep on the heavy

31

carpet. Rolling his eyes, he saw the English guard had returned. He glanced at the bunks, then began his slow, maddening pacing up and down the floor.

Once, he stopped before Trask's bunk and stood there chuckling. "You will not have much longer to disclose the name of the inventor," he said. "If you do not wish to be the first to be experimented upon by the Murder Machine, be ready to tell what you know when the Master returns."

Again that slow pacing. Minutes ticking by.

The place was lighted dimly by two Chinese lamps that stood on pedestals at opposite corners of the room.

Suddenly the lights went out. Hazard at the same time sensed a prickling feeling in his legs and arms. The narcotic was wearing off. He had begun to have a slight hope of working out of the ropes that held him.

Now in the darkness, he struggled frantically. Yes, he could feel thongs cut into his wrists. But they were tight, horribly so.

Out of the blackness came sounds. The sound of feet moving fast. That would be the Englishman, rushing to see why the lights had gone out.

The footsteps sounded louder. There was a bump and a thud. Likely, the guard had collided with a stand in the darkness—or perhaps the side of the room.

But there was no outcry, not even a mumbled curse.

More footsteps. The sound of them made Hazard's flesh crawl. Something was being dragged across the floor hurriedly. And all this time, Jerry Hazard was fighting like mad. His strength was returning rapidly. He thought he felt one of the turns of rope loosen just a little.

Savagely, he fought with his hands to follow up the cords to where they were fastened to the wall. They were looped through a great iron ring there.

Vainly he tried to find the knot where they were tied. Must be at his wrists. He couldn't feel any joining of the ropes with his fingers. Didn't have the freedom of his hands to get the fingers near enough to his wrists, to feel there.

All grew still inside the opium den. He struggled on. One, two minutes crawled by.

His ears were suddenly ringing with a new sound. The faint jabbering of Cantonese talk far off—muffled and strange.

Bam!

Hazard gave a violent start as the lights were turned on.

The room was empty. A feeling of horror surged through Hazard. Perhaps he was here alone. That dragging on the floor must have been Wu Fang's attendants taking Gerald Trask out for his experiment. But why hadn't he cried out in fear and torture? Perhaps—

Hazard couldn't hold in longer. He raised his voice. It came huskily, and the sound of it was strange, even to him.

"Trask! Are you there?"

"Ye-yes," came an instant answer. "Are you there?"

"Right. What happened while the lights were turned off?"

"I—don't know. I thought they were taking you out or—"

He raised his voice slightly: "Kildare!"

But only the sullen sound of his voice came back to him.

33

Hazard stiffened with another thought. Perhaps they had taken Kildare out of his bunk.

His brain began spinning once more. Round and round like a top, touching lightly on every thought, every fear that had come to him during the time he lay there.

Minutes dragged like hours, making the suspense almost more than he could bear without going stark, raving mad. Mohra back in Wu Fang's power. Kildare probably dead. And death staring him in the face as soon as the yellow fiend finished constructing the Murder Machine.

HIS BRAIN went spinning again. The room swam before his eyes. Then it stopped and his bulging eyes focused on one thing.

It was a tall yellow man, with narrow, slightly bent shoulders and green eyes. It was Wu Fang, smiling.

The long-nailed hands clapped as a signal. From somewhere far off that same dignified, deep gong sounded.

Bonggggg!

The very air inside the stuffy room shuddered with the vibration.

Wu Fang stepped to the side of the opium den opposite the row of bunks. He turned expectantly, his eyes on the heavy oriental hangings that covered the wall at the end of the room.

The tapestries moved ever so slightly.

But slowly, surely, they were parting. A rumbling sound filled the room.

Something was being wheeled in by two slant-eyed Chinese.

Instantly Hazard grasped the answer. It was the Murder Machine.

The Dragon Lord of Crime stepped before the machine's advance and held out one hand. It stopped. Then he spoke.

"You will attach the cord that furnishes power to the apparatus," he commanded.

He turned to Hazard with a sweeping glance past the bunk where as yet no sound had come from Kildare.

"I regret that the lights went out," he said. "But perhaps the darkness aided you in thinking your last thoughts." His green eyes glinted as they shot about the place. "Where is Wallace?" he demanded.

His eyes were riveted on Jerry Hazard.

"Wallace, the English agent I left on guard here?"

"If I knew," Hazard snapped, "I wouldn't tell you."

He did some quick thinking.

"But if you really want to know," he said, "he has gone to warn the real inventor of the device against you, you yellow devil."

Wu Fang's eyes glowed brighter. It was a horrible sight—as though the man's eyes were lighted from inside by electricity.

"You are a liar, Mr. Hazard," he said.

He turned back to the machine. His hands unclasped and extended toward the black cloth that covered it. With a deft stroke, he drew aside the covering just a little.

Hazard gaped. A small snout projected from the cloth, not unlike the large end of a telescope. There was a hood extending for six inches that was hollow, but inside, he saw the light reflected upon a glass.

He was thinking back to Kildare's description of what he knew of the device. It was very little. But from what the government man had said he had guessed that it was some sort of death-ray machine.

Wu Fang was speaking in his singsong tongue which Hazard couldn't understand. Two Chinese attendants leaped to obey. Together they strode toward Hazard's bunk. Had the devil changed his mind? Was he going to take Hazard first?

But they moved on past that middle bunk toward Gerald Trask. Hazard turned his head, trying to follow their movements. But the partition between the bunks hid them from view.

Trask's voice, cracked and strained, came to him.

"For the love of Heaven, don't kill me. I—"

There was the sound of struggling. The two Chinese, with Trask fighting between them, were coming into the range of Hazard's vision. Trask was scared beyond description. His eyes protruded. His face was white, like wood ashes. His mouth was open and his throat moved. But no words came from his lips, as the two stout Chinese agents dragged him before Wu Fang.

"The time has come," Wu Fang was saying, "for you to make an important decision, Mr. Gerald Trask. I wish to know the name of the inventor who is experimenting to improve this Murder Machine. I want also the address where he can be found."

Wu Fang stopped. The fingers of his extended hands widened.

"Tell me the name," he cooed softly.

Hazard was straining at his ropes.

"Don't tell," he shouted. "Don't tell, if you value the life of every—"

But there he was cut off. Wu Fang whirled upon him, so swiftly that Hazard couldn't follow his movements.

Long-nailed, powerfully fingered hands were at his throat. The strength of this crime master was appalling. When Wu Fang let up his pressure and backed away a step, Hazard found it impossible to do more than gasp and stare.

"PERHAPS IT is better this way," Wu Fang said. "I had not thought of it before; but if Mr. Trask were to see you subjected to the machine of death, if he saw your writhings and torture, he would tell me what I wish to know more readily."

Wu Fang spoke rapidly in Cantonese to the two that held Trask. The young banker was returned to his bunk.

Things swam dizzily before Hazard. He was to be next. The Chinese aides were before him now, untying his ropes.

He relaxed, forcing himself to go limp. This was his last chance. If he could pull a surprise that would be devastating, then—

He closed his eyes. Felt that he was free now. They were lifting him bodily out of the bunk. Standing him up. Dragging him across the floor.

If he ever moved swiftly, it must be now.

Now!

With that thought he opened his eyes. At the same time he threw himself backward with all the force at his command.

The surprise did the trick. He tore himself loose from the

Wu Fang was standing with
his arms raised in surrender.

grasp of the two yellow brutes. He was free. Free for at least a
split second.

Wham!

As he caught himself, he lunged forward. One of the Chinese
aides was lunging for him. Hazard let go a right that had all
the desperation he felt behind it. The blow was perfect.

Another agent was coming in. Powerful hands were groping

38

for Hazard. The newspaperman ducked and weaved and struck again.

Bam!

A left caught that oriental on the cheek and half turned his head. But it didn't have the affect of the first blow on the other.

Wu Fang was screaming; then he came tearing in himself.

An opening. Hazard took it. He had had his eyes on the

drape from behind which he and Kildare had been dragged into the opium den. That would surely be an exit.

Head down, shoulders hunched forward, Hazard lunged for that spot. His fists were flailing as he plunged straight for Wu Fang and his aide.

Unk!

The aide grunted and doubled as Hazard smashed him in the stomach.

Wu Fang, screaming still, was on his left. Hazard leaped for him, left arm extended. But something happened in that split second. Wu Fang darted away from his reach and left Hazard fighting to regain his balance.

Then he was going down, and someone was beating him over the head. Stars blinked and everything swam before his eyes. He was still struggling, but it was of no use. He had had his chance. The odds had been too great.

The room was filled with yellow devils, jabbering and grinning. They were dragging him hurriedly before the machine. From somewhere a dull thudding sound came to his ears.

"Tie him to the ceiling. Quickly," Wu Fang ordered.

A rope was being fastened about his wrists. He was jerked off his feet, left hanging in the air, and foul hands were tearing the clothing from his body.

Many things flashed before his eyes in that brief last moment. The slumped figure in Kildare's bunk, lying still, as though life had left it forever, face to the wall.

Trask was staring with bulging eyes from his bunk.

Wu Fang stood a little away, hand raised in signal. His agents leaped back to a corner of the room. One lone Chinaman, small and alert, with an intelligent face, stood beside the black-robed machine. The snout was pointed at Hazard's half-naked body.

"When I lower my hand, the machine will be turned on."

That was Wu Fang's last command.

Hazard's eyes felt like two burning balls of fire. They were riveted on Wu Fang's arm. The arm of death. It was moving.

"Wu Fang!" Hazard cried. "One last request. If you—"

The arm of the yellow fiend fell.

Bam!

CHAPTER 4
DRAGNET JUSTICE

THERE WAS sudden wild confusion. Something sputtered from the machine that the black cloth shrouded.

Hazard sensed a strange light settling on him. The light had no color as far as he could tell. Then his skin began to feel as though a torch had been applied.

But there were other sounds that he caught, even through the awful pain of the death ray.

Blam! Blam!

There was a great commotion outside the room. Heavy pounding on the walls. At the same time the Orientals and brown men chattered out an unearthly jibbering.

Wu Fang whirled and rushed out of Hazard's sight.

Crash!

Something went down with a bang. It might have been a

heavy door or the whole side of the room. But Hazard was too much in torment now to care.

A voice cracked out above the stampede.

"Don't move, or I'll shoot!"

It was Val Kildare's voice.

Hazard was burning. The pain was so great that he could only writhe. But his eyes, staring ahead, were riveted—bulging—on the bunk where they had laid Kildare. There was the limp form with the broad shoulders, still there. And the face was still turned away from him.

All of these things took but a few seconds. Someone sprang past him with a shout.

"Keep 'em covered!"

Wham!

There was a crash, and the machine of death was hurled back through the drapes. Blue flashes lighted the room. The lights had gone out. Men were shouting. Those shouts were from Britishers.

Except for the intermittent electric arcing, the room was dark. Then a wall of flame shot up before Hazard. An arm was about him and a reassuring voice was saying:

"It's okay, Jerry. It's me. I'm cutting you down. Hold—"

Blam! Blam! Blam!

Out of the corner of his eye Hazard saw three forms topple over. He was falling to the floor. That same arm was holding him. He managed to turn his head. It was Kildare.

Hazard breathed the name weakly.

"How did you—" he started to say, but Kildare cut him off.

"Never mind that. I'll explain everything. Here, Inspector, take care of Hazard. Get the others untied. Got to get out of here, or we'll be burned to a crisp."

Eager hands were bearing Jerry Hazard through the smoke-laden room. Hazard tried to fight free. There was something else that even his tortured, tangled body couldn't let him forget.

"Get Wu Fang," he cried. "He was—"

He stopped. Gasped for breath. Wu Fang was standing in the smoke with three Scotland Yard men holding their guns at his back. Some of his agents lay dead. Others were held at bay by the police of London.

Kildare turned to face the yellow fiend, but Wu Fang spoke first.

"You would like to shoot me where I stand, Mr. Kildare," he smiled. "But unfortunately, I have my hands raised over my head. You see, most honorable sir, I completely surrender as your prisoner."

In that dim view, Hazard saw Kildare's face turn a light shade of purple. The muscles of the government man's jaw bulged as he clenched his teeth.

"Yes, confound it," Kildare rasped, "you surrender! I wish to heaven that you'd tried to escape. But if there's justice in this world, you yellow devil, you'll hang to the highest scaffold in England."

Kildare half-turned as Hazard was carried out the door. Flames crackled, and the place was intensely hot. Kildare uttered a command to get out of the place while there was time. But

Hazard couldn't see anything more of him or of Wu Fang or the agents and police who were coming from the fire-swept pit.

Through dark passages they carried him. The pain of burning in his skin had lessened a little. Flashlight gleams danced before their advance.

"I think," Hazard ventured, "if you'll set me on my feet, I can make a go of it."

He was carried a little farther. Then they stood him up after climbing a short, steep stairs of stone steps. His legs wobbled unsteadily; but, with the help of an Inspector who took hold of his arm, he managed to move along at a good pace.

More steps, and out into the fog-drenched night. With an inspector walking on either side of him, they hurried down the dark, narrow street.

Despite his strange burns and pain, Hazard was filled with boundless joy. Wu Fang and most of his agents were captured, which meant the end of the reign of the Dragon Lord of Crime. Then suddenly he remembered the news of Mohra's capture in New York. The whole thing seemed so unreal. Yet perhaps Wu Fang was lying, knowing such false news of Mohra's imprisonment would make his torture all the more unbearable.

Then the two inspectors were pushing him into a car that stood waiting in the second block. "To the hospital at once," one ordered.

Jerry Hazard straightened. "No," he argued. "I'll be all right. Take me to police headquarters, where Wu Fang is going. The police surgeon can look me over there. There's something I've got to attend to at once."

"Very well, to headquarters we go," the inspector who was driving decided.

The car rolled off, feeling its way slowly through the fog. Minutes later, they entered headquarters.

Inside the great office, Hazard saw Kildare coming at the head of a group of Scotland Yard men. At least a dozen guns were showing, and in the center of the group, heavily manacled but smiling calmly, walked Wu Fang.

Typical Englishman that he was, the Chief Inspector of the Yard surveyed the master criminal calmly. He nodded to Kildare.

"Very commendable work, sir," he said.

"Thank you," Kildare replied.

Then the government man turned his attention to Hazard.

"I thought I ordered you to the hospital, Jerry."

"You did," Hazard admitted, "but I had to come over here. I thought the police surgeon could look me over. I'll be all right. I've got some things that need immediate attention."

Kildare shrugged.

"All right," he said. He turned back to the Chief Inspector. "You'll have the surgeon look at Hazard at once?" he asked.

HAZARD WENT reluctantly. He didn't want to leave Wu Fang. He hesitated at the door, turned back, eyeing Kildare. But the government man nodded reassuringly.

"It's all right, Jerry," he said. "Don't worry about Wu Fang. We've got him, and if it is humanly possible, we're going to keep him until we can dangle him at the end of a rope."

The surgeon followed him in, made a careful examination. He was frowning as he did so.

"This ray or light or whatever it was," he asked. "How long was it directed on you?"

Hazard tried to think.

"Just a few seconds," he said. "I'm sure it wasn't any longer than that."

The doctor had his watch out at the moment, feeling Hazard's heartbeats.

"There," Hazard said. "Just about like that, I believe. That's about three seconds, possibly four."

The surgeon nodded and continued his examination.

"Fortunate for you," he said, "that it wasn't any longer. "Were you standing naked before the machine?"

"Why, no," Hazard said. "They only stripped me to the waist."

"That's strange," the doctor said, shaking his head. "From what I can see, your clothing didn't protect you any." He rubbed his hand hard over Hazard's skin. "How does that feel?" he asked.

"Not any too pleasant," Hazard admitted.

"As near as I can make out," the surgeon concluded, "you have a severe attack of sunburn. At least that's what I would call it if I hadn't heard about the machine."

"Sunburn?" Hazard repeated. "You mean even through my clothes?"

"Exactly," said the surgeon. "I think we caught it in time, though. You know, if three-quarters of the body becomes badly sunburned, it is apt to cause insanity of the worst kind. Attacks the nerve tips near the surface of the skin, you know. I'll rub on some healing ointment that will cure you."

As Hazard returned to the larger room, he saw that it was nearly empty. The

Chief Inspector was no longer at his desk. He heard voices coming from a partially opened door beyond, made his way over there.

Wu Fang was in the center of the room, surrounded by Scotland Yard men, all with their guns aimed directly at him.

The yellow fiend was being ruthlessly searched and questioned, but always there was that calm, cool smile on the thin lips. He laughed softly when a question came from the Chief Inspector.

"All this is quite childish, honorable Chief Inspector," he said. "You go through this because you do not know me. I believe you will have no trouble in convicting me on charges serious enough so that you may have the privilege of hanging me."

Hazard pushed his way through the throng of inspectors, past Kildare and Gerald Trask.

"You yellow devil," he rasped, his voice shaking with desperate earnestness, "you're going to send orders to your agents in New York's Chinatown to release Mohra."

Again Wu Fang laughed. Laughed derisively in the newspaperman's face.

"You should know me better than that, Mr. Hazard," he said. "Wu Fang gives orders; he does not obey them."

Hazard's fist clenched. He started for the tall, gaunt, chuckling yellow man, but a hand caught his arm and jerked him back.

"Take it easy, Jerry," Kildare advised. "We would all like to tear the rat apart, but unfortunately, we must abide by the law."

The Dragon Lord of Crime stiffened; the smile fled from his face.

"I may be your prisoner," he said haughtily, "but I do not have to tolerate sarcastic insults. Take me to my cell."

Kildare bowed and smiled.

"It is a pleasure, I assure you," he said.

Jerry Hazard marched in the long procession down the corridor to a double cell, one within the other. There was a clanking of steel, a creak of heavy hinges, and Wu Fang passed into confinement as the inner and outer doors were both securely locked behind him.

Kildare turned to the Chief Inspector.

"If I might suggest," he said, "there should be at least three guards outside at all times."

"Never fear," the Chief Inspector smiled. "No one has ever escaped from this cell, and no one ever will."

Back at the Chief's desk, Kildare shook hands with him.

"You know my hotel address," he said. "If anything should turn up, call me immediately."

The Chief Inspector looked puzzled.

"Anything should turn up?" he repeated. "But, I say, what have you in mind? We have Wu Fang in a double cell and he's heavily guarded."

Kildare merely shrugged in answer. He turned and glanced at Gerald Trask.

"IT MAY be that for the rest of the night, we'll be at Mr.

Trask's residence," he said. Then to Trask, "You live alone with your father?"

Young Trask nodded.

"You don't mind if we see you to your home and look things over a bit, do you?"

"No, indeed," Trask said, looking very much relieved. "I'd be honored, I'm sure."

"Then," said Kildare to the Chief Inspector, "if you can't get us at our hotel, you'll find us at Trask's."

"I believe, Inspector," Hazard said, "you can get a cablegram through faster than the usual channels will carry it."

The Chief Inspector nodded.

"A cablegram?" Kildare asked.

"Yes," Hazard told him. "I want to hear from Mohra. I have a hunch that Wu Fang was lying about her."

Kildare smiled mysteriously.

"I don't think he lied to you, Jerry," he said, "but I think he was mistaken."

"What do you mean?" Hazard demanded quickly.

"I may be wrong," Kildare said, "so I don't want to get your hopes up. If I'm correct, you'll know very shortly."

Hazard eyed the government man in perplexity. Then he turned to the desk, picked up a blank sheet of paper and scribbled the cable on it.

"You want this to go to the police in New York?" the Chief Inspector asked.

"If you please," Hazard nodded. "And as quickly as possible. Tell them I want an answer at once."

As their cab ploughed through the thick mist on its way to the Trask mansion, Val Kildare explained how he had tricked Wu Fang.

"You see, Jerry," he said, "when I learned that we were both being followed, after we had found the two dead inspectors, I knew immediately that we were pretty well surrounded by agents of Wu Fang. I tried to get you to leave me, Jerry, but you didn't, and you nearly paid with your life for it."

"I couldn't leave you lying there on the ground, helpless, and stunned by the narcotic," Hazard said. "I thought you were dead."

Kildare smiled.

"So I fooled you too, did I?"

"Why, yes," Hazard said. "Weren't you knocked out by the narcotic?"

"No," Kildare told him. "It didn't touch me. I waited until I heard the sound of the dart leaving the sarbacan, or blow pipe. I dropped just in time so that the drugged dart missed me. The agent who was following you must have gotten you a moment later. I saw you fall, but I didn't dare move."

"You mean," Trask demanded, "that you deliberately let them capture you?"

Kildare nodded.

"Yes," he said, "that was the only way I could find out where Wu Fang's hiding place was located. This was my last resort. I knew I would be taken to Wu Fang if I was captured."

"But how on earth," Hazard demanded, "did you get out of

there? When I last saw you, you were lying in your bunk, tied fast."

"When they bound me to the back of the bunk," Kildare said, "they thought I didn't know what was going on, so it was quite simple for me to keep my muscles taut. Then when I relaxed, the ropes were loose. I worked my arms and legs free after quite a bit of struggling. You remember when the lights went out?"

"I'll never forget it," Trask said, shivering a little.

"I succeeded in knocking out Wu Fang's English agent, whom I think he called Wallace. I put him in my place in the bunk with his face to the wall as mine had been. Apparently, he looked enough like me so that the illusion was successful. Then, of course, the rest was very simple. If I had dared, I would have released you too and taken you with me, but that would have wrecked everything. Wu Fang would have known that something was up, and when I got back with the Scotland Yard men, he wouldn't have been there. Now we have him in a double cell and heaven knows he's going to stay there until they hang him."

The home of the great London banker occupied one half of a city block in the residential section. In the thinning fog they could see the large stone structure looming in the darkness like a ghostly, strange monster. It was entirely surrounded by a high, iron spiked fence.

As they walked through the gate, Kildare was scrutinizing the mansion carefully. It was a veritable fortress, with every window barred.

The great iron gates jangled eerily in the gloom as a man-servant closed and locked them from the inside. One of the doors before them opened ponderously, and a butler bowed.

"Good evening, sir," he said to Gerald Trask, who strode in past him, followed by Kildare and Hazard.

"Your father just returned an hour ago, if I may say so, sir," the butler ventured.

Gerald Trask showed instant relief. "I am very glad to hear that," he said. "Has he retired?"

"I believe so. Do you wish me to tell him that you are back, sir?"

Young Trask glanced at Kildare, saw the government man nod.

"Yes," he said. "Tell him I have some friends who would like very much to see him."

The butler bowed, and turning, went stiffly up the great staircase that curved out of the vaulted reception hall.

Kildare frowned.

"You have a butler on duty at all hours, morning and night?" he asked.

"Yes," the young banker admitted. "Except for the kitchen help, we have two complete staffs of house servants. They are on duty twelve hours apiece."

"I see," Kildare nodded.

Trask hesitated, glanced at the several arched doorways that led from the hall. He half-turned toward one of them.

"I want my father to meet you," he said. "After all, you've saved my life. I believe we will be more comfortable in the—"

TRASK NEVER finished that sentence. An ear-splitting scream sounded from above.

Kildare jumped as though a giant spring had been touched off within him and rushed headlong up the stairs, crying, "Come on! There's no time to lose."

Again the scream came, shrill and terror-stricken.

"Trask, quick! Get up here and show me which room belongs to your father!"

The scream sounded a third time. All too slowly Trask realized its horrible significance.

"Down the hall, first door on the left," he cried. "Father! Father!"

With one stroke of his hand, Kildare swept the servant from in front of the door.

"Come on, Jerry," he cried.

Hazard knew what was expected of him as the government man drew back from the door, his shoulders bent forward.

"One, two, three!" Kildare counted in quick succession.

The two of them charged with all their might against the door. It bulged but held. A gasping, choking cry came from the other side.

"One, two, three!"

Wham!

Perfect teamwork that time. There was a crashing sound as they collided with the door and it burst inward. A shadowy form darted past Hazard. It was Kildare fumbling in the dark, crying, "The light! Where's that confounded light?"

There came the snap of a switch, and the room was instantly illuminated by a dim, shaded glow.

Hazard saw Kildare turn his head quickly, knew that the government man had taken everything in with one swift sweep of his eyes.

The newspaperman was a little slower in seeing things. One of the windows was open. He could see a grotesque form outside in the gray mist. For the first instant that his eyes lighted upon it, he was tempted to cry out. Then he realized that it was the leafy branch of a tree hanging outside the window.

There were spots of red on the windowsill and stains of the same bloody color on the floor. On the bed, with the covers partly drawn back, was the figure of a portly, gray-haired man.

Gerald Trask was rushing toward him, crying, "Father! Father!"

Hazard watched him for a moment, let his eyes travel on around the room. A picture on the wall was tilted at a peculiar angle on one end.

Kildare was running toward the window, shouting, "The robber escaped this way! Lucky thing those new plans were in the main safe in the basement."

Hazard's brows knit together in perplexity, and his eyes narrowed. What was Kildare talking about?

Gerald Trask was frantically shaking his father's shoulders. Kildare jerked his head to Hazard, motioned toward the door, and nodded to young Trask. Very gently, he lifted the young banker off the bed.

"Come on, Trask," he said, "I'm afraid there's nothing you

can do here. It will be best if you go downstairs. I'll give you all the details after I have made a thorough investigation."

Young Trask stood up, tense, mute.

"I'm mighty sorry," Hazard said, taking him by the arm. "Kildare's right. Let's go downstairs."

Without a word, Trask permitted himself to be led out into the hall and down the great staircase. Hazard took him into the library, where they had been going when that awful scream came.

Trask was staring fixedly straight ahead. Hazard took a cigarette from a box on the table and put it between the man's lips.

"Thanks—so much," the young banker said as Hazard lighted it for him.

Hazard turned to go, but Trask stopped him.

"You will tell me as soon as you find out anything?" he asked.

"Yes," Hazard nodded. "Try to take it easy."

Trask licked his lips. "If money—anything—will do any good—" he began.

"I'll let you know," Hazard promised.

He turned quickly and strode out of the room. He plunged up the stairs two at a time and dashed into the bedchamber of Bertrand Trask.

Kildare was standing in the center of the room, staring about. Hazard rushed back to the bed for a closer scrutiny. The bed clothing, both about the figure and the head, was smeared with blood. The throat of Trask, Senior, was a gory sight, red and wet and horrible.

55

But the thing that caused Hazard to stop and catch his breath in utter amazement was the print of a foot, clear and well-defined on the counterpane.

"Good Lord," he breathed. "Kildare, did you see this?"

He turned his head, saw Kildare nod.

"You mean the bloody print of a baby's foot?" the government man asked.

CHAPTER 5
THE CLIMBING HORROR

HAZARD SPUN around as though he had received an electric jolt. He stared down again at that lone footprint. Yes, that was it. The footprint of a baby or a very small child on the pure white of the bed-covering. It was red with blood, mingled with specks of dirt.

"What does it mean?" he demanded. "Is it a sign like a black hand?"

"No," Kildare said.

That was all he would offer for the moment.

Hazard's eyes shifted to the throat of the corpse.

"But a baby couldn't have done that," he said. "It—"

"Wait," Kildare interrupted him. And then a moment later, "No, you're right, Jerry. I think I've got it. Come over and stand by me. No, on this side. Not too close to the window. There's no telling what might happen if you expose yourself. Where did you leave Trask?"

"In the library," Hazard answered.

Kildare nodded.

"That's as safe a place as any," he said. "We'll go down there in a minute. Look here." He pointed to the windowsill. "You see, there are marks of blood there. Unfortunately, the rug is predominantly red and the blood doesn't show up very clearly. But if you look carefully you can see a few tracks leading across it."

He pointed to the picture that was strangely cocked on the wall. The butler was standing in the doorway dumbfounded and tongue-tied. Hazard caught a glimpse of him out of the corner of his eye, saw him try to get a grip on himself.

"Is there anything I can—?" the manservant stammered.

"No," Kildare replied. "Go down to the library and see what you can do for young Trask. If you have a gun, get it out and be ready for anything."

The butler bowed and started down the hall.

"Tell the other servants not to leave the house," Kildare called after him.

Kildare strode over to the picture and lifted it. Now Hazard saw what had caused it to stand out from the wall at such a strange angle. There was an ample safe hidden behind it. The door had been left open, causing the picture to tilt outward. They saw immediately that the safe was empty.

As Kildare gingerly closed the little door, Hazard noticed there was blood on the knob of the dial and on the open handle. The government man pointed to the dresser that stood near to the safe. On the top of it was the print of a baby's foot, also in blood.

Kildare seemed to be judging the distance between the dresser and the safe, a distance that Hazard guessed was perhaps two feet. The government man turned quickly. "So he had his throat torn out, did he, Jerry?"

Hazard stared past him toward the bed.

"Why, yes," he said. "Look for yourself. See all the blood on—"

He stopped short as he saw Kildare stroke the wrinkled throat of the elderly man.

"Try it for yourself, Jerry," he invited. "There's so much blood around the throat that you can't see very much. I'll have you made mayor of London if you can find a break in the skin."

Hazard stroked the throat through the smear of blood, drew back quickly.

"Good Lord!" he breathed. "What's the answer, Kildare? His throat is just as whole as yours or mine. Where did all this blood come from?"

Kildare jerked his head toward the window.

"From there," he said. "I've learned that much now. Let's go downstairs. I don't want to leave young Trask alone too long."

Trask was puffing nervously on the cigarette that Hazard had lighted for him. His eyes stared pleadingly. "Is he—dead?"

Kildare placed a comforting hand on his shoulder.

"Yes, Trask," he said. "Your father was strangled."

"Strangled! But the blood! You mean—"

"I examined your father's body thoroughly," Kildare told him. "There was no mark anywhere, no sign of skin broken."

"But the blood," Trask repeated frantically. "I don't understand."

"I'm not sure about that angle of it myself as yet," Kildare said. "There's only one explanation that I can think of. That fence around the ground is topped with very sharp spikes, isn't it?"

"Why, yes, but—"

"Whatever was in that room," Kildare continued, "had to get either through or over that fence."

"You mean," Hazard blurted out, "that the one who caused the murder was injured in climbing over the fence?"

"That's the best I can do so far," Kildare said. "In other words, it is his blood and not Mr. Trask's that's spattered about the bedroom."

The government man turned to the banker's son.

"As we came in, I noticed that you had quite an ample basement under the house," he said. "Are the windows there barred like these up above?"

Trask, still very much stunned, nodded dumbly.

"Give me the layout of the basement," Kildare suggested.

"Well, there really isn't very much to it," Trask said. "The boiler by which the house is heated is in the center of the largest space. Then there are two other rooms partitioned off. One is for storage and the other is the laundry. But"—his eyes narrowed as he stared harder at Kildare—"I say, didn't I hear you mention a larger safe in the basement when you went to close my father's window?"

"Yes," Kildare said. "I'm coming to that."

"But look here," Trask argued. "There's no safe in the basement."

"I didn't really imagine that there was," Kildare admitted.

"But you said—"

"I was merely laying a little trap for our visitor," Kildare told him. "About that safe in your father's room. Was there anything there?"

Trask shook his head.

"I DON'T think so," he said, "unless there might have been a few old papers. That was where father and I kept the formula of the death machine. Of course, you understand we guarded it very zealously because we knew what would happen if it should fall into the hands of an unscrupulous person like this Wu Fang."

"I know," Kildare nodded shortly. He moved a little closer to Trask. "Look here, Trask," he said. "Your father is dead now. We're all deeply grieved, I can assure you, but we haven't reached the end of the trail yet by any means. As a matter of fact, I'm afraid we've only begun. Suppose you tell me all about this thing from the start to the finish."

"I believe you know almost everything," Trask said. "You see, the inventor of this death machine has been conducting a series of experiments. After he completed his first machine, he needed money to go on. The British government would have gladly furnished him the needed capital, but then, you see, in that case, he would have been working for them, and when he finished his invention, they might have taken it over."

Kildare frowned perplexedly, and Trask rushed on to explain.

Trask's throat was a gory sight, red and wet and horrible.

"It's not that I'm criticizing my own empire," he said quickly. "But you see, in the British government, as in that of almost every other nation, you are apt to find unscrupulous politicians who are in search of glory for themselves. Some high officials would not hesitate to do the inventor out of his rights to this machine if they thought they could benefit themselves by it."

"Yes," Kildare admitted. "That might happen in any nation. I assume that the inventor came to you and your father and you agreed to finance him."

"Exactly," Trask nodded. "That made it a private affair. The inventor insisted upon putting up as collateral the plans of his first machine. Those plans are what I was tricked into bringing to the opium den. However, the machine that was built from those plans was not nearly as effective as the inventor expected it to be; so my father and I loaned him money for further development. He's working on it now."

Kildare snapped out a one-word question so quickly that it caught young Trask partially off guard.

"Where?" he demanded.

"At our—"

Young Trask's lips closed firmly after those two words, and his face flushed.

"That, Mr. Kildare," he said, "is something I promised my father never to divulge. Neither that nor the name of the inventor."

Kildare smiled.

"It's perfectly all right, Trask," he said. "I understand. I take it that the inventor is now working on something that is going to be effective, let us say, in time of war."

Trask dismissed the butler and closed the library door before he answered.

"I can tell you this much," he said. "The death machine that Wu Fang used on Mr. Hazard was quite ineffectual compared to this new apparatus. The machine you saw was simply a slight elaboration on an X-ray device with a special chemical used in the filament. The inventor is searching for something that will kill instantly and at great range. I can assure you that his experiments are practically completed. He expects to make a demonstration at any time."

Suddenly, Trask stiffened and his lips formed a tight line across his even teeth.

"I have told you all that I can for the time being, Mr. Kildare," he said. "And I believe you promised to tell me something."

"Yes," Kildare admitted in a kindly voice. "But first, may I ask you one more question, Trask. That wall safe in your father's room wasn't used a great deal, was it?"

"No," the banker's son answered.

"Therefore it was necessary for you to carry the combination of the safe on a slip of paper in your wallet?"

"Yes," Trask admitted. He began fumbling in his pockets. A blank expression suddenly crossed his face as his hands found nothing there.

"It's gone!" he cried. "They must have taken my wallet when they captured me."

"I haven't the least doubt of it," Kildare said. "That just about completes my story of what happened upstairs. You see, Trask, Wu Fang knew that this inventor to whom you have loaned money is working on a much more deadly machine than the one that he used on Jerry.

"When you were captured, his men searched you and found the combination of the safe where you had kept the plans of the machine. It's highly probable, in my mind, that Wu Fang counted on the possibility that there was a plan of the new machine in the safe which perhaps you didn't dare take out of the house for any reason, so he sent for it.

"His agent, in climbing over the high-spiked fence, got cut or gashed so that he bled profusely. Nevertheless, he came on, got into your father's room through the window, and went straight to the safe, paying no attention to Mr. Trask.

"He was at the safe, opening it, when the butler knocked at the door. That awakened your father, and immediately the visitor leaped from the bureau to the floor, choked him to death, and escaped through the window, leaving a trail of blood wherever he went.

"If that theory is correct, Trask, he'll be returning very shortly—to the basement. I personally want to be there as chairman of the reception committee. How about you, Jerry?"

Hazard nodded and moved toward the door. Trask's teeth clenched.

"You can count me in too," he said. He drew out the drawer of a great, carved desk, took an automatic from it and turned toward the door.

"I'm ready," he said grimly. "I'd give all I have for the opportunity of getting the murderer of my father."

"You may have him for nothing, if he comes," Kildare replied.

The government man ordered no lights turned on in the basement; but he did procure an electric torch from the butler before going downstairs.

"You know the basement pretty well, Trask?" he asked as the young banker opened the door.

"Yes." Trask nodded tensely.

Hazard saw Kildare glance at the young banker's gun.

"Be a little careful of that," he suggested. "Don't shoot until you're pretty sure it's what you want to kill."

TRASK MADE no answer. He turned and started down the stairs very softly, one step at a time. Kildare went next, and Hazard brought up the rear.

"No noise now," Kildare whispered. "Close that door, Jerry. We don't want any light down here."

Hazard obeyed, and they were instantly plunged into total darkness.

"We'll move over to the right, Trask," Kildare said softly. "I want a position directly below your father's bedroom window, the one that was open."

Soft padding of feet moving cautiously on the concrete floor, the slight creak of a door.

"Sssh," Kildare warned.

"This is the storage room," Trask whispered. "It's directly below father's room, two stories down, of course."

"Follow close," the government man whispered. "I've got

hold of Trask. We don't want to kick against any boxes or trunks. Some of those creatures of Wu Fang have an uncanny sense of hearing and sight."

As Hazard's eyes became more accustomed to the darkness, he saw there were two windows along an upper wall of the basement, placed about six feet apart. Both were heavily barred.

As he went on, he could make out the vague outlines of boxes and trunks and old furniture heaped about the place. He realized there was some light coming through those two high-up windows from the outside, reflected from the street lamps. The fog must be lifting, he decided.

He heard Kildare ask Trask, "Are those windows fastened on the inside?"

"Yes," Trask breathed, "but I don't know just how."

"It doesn't matter," Kildare whispered back.

Minutes dragged slowly by. The only sound was the muffled breathing of the three men. The almost inaudible respiration of Kildare and Hazard and the more labored effort of Trask.

Suddenly, Hazard felt Kildare pulling him down to a crouched position beside a trunk. He could sense the government man's tension. Hazard strained his eyes toward those windows, strained his ears to listen.

Was there a sound or was it merely his imagination? The crackling of a twig perhaps. Kildare was rising a little. There was a sound; Jerry Hazard was sure of it now. A gentle swish outside that window to the right, as though a branch had been softly pulled aside and allowed to swing back in place.

Hazard brought his gun up. Something was just outside the

window but not yet visible. He thought dawn was near. Yes, it was slowly growing lighter outside.

Something moved on the other side of the bars. Was it a branch? Or was it a living being? Hazard couldn't be sure. He was taking aim as best he could in the dark.

Blam! And then a split second later, *blam!*

The roar of the two guns was deafening. Hazard pulled his trigger, and his own gun boomed. There was a wild crashing of shattered glass, and a choked cry like the scream of a child rent the air, subsiding in a convulsive sob.

Kildare's flashlight went on, and he was tearing for the door.

"Come on!" he cried, plunging up the stairs three steps at a time.

It was all Hazard could do to follow him. Trask was right behind the newspaperman, trying to hurry him forward. Kildare burst into the upper hall and paused a moment.

"Is there a door on the side, Trask?" he asked.

Trask raced past, shouting, "Yes, follow me."

They ran through the dining room into a conservatory. Trask was fumbling frantically, trying to get a door unlocked. He made it and darted out.

"Here!" Trask cried. "Here's the place."

The beam of Kildare's light swept instantly to a small clump of shrubbery at the base of the mansion. Trask was there a few feet ahead of them. A cry of astonishment came from his lips.

"I say, look here," he cried. "I never—"

To Hazard, it looked at first like a child. A child whose body was covered for the most part with a growth of skimpy hair instead of clothing. But the face was not that of a child. It was less human than that. The jaw protruded like that of a monkey; the lips were thick, and the nose flat. The eyes were small and round and had a glassy stare. A mass of slippery blood covered the little body where the bullet had stabbed it. The muscles still twitched slightly as the final breath of life left the animal.

Kildare grabbed hold of the little body by the nape of the neck and dragged it out on the lawn.

"I say," Trask exploded. "You mean to tell me that that—whatever you may call it—is what killed my father?"

They could see the thing quite clearly now in the light of the breaking dawn.

WITHOUT ANSWERING Trask's question, Kildare picked up one of the little creature's feet. It was exactly like the foot of a small child. The legs were short and stocky. From head to heels, the thing couldn't have measured more than three feet. But the arms, although they grew from thin, immature shoulders, were long and powerful, with fingers of steel.

"But I say, I never saw anything like it before in my life," Trask cried. "It can't be a monkey. It hasn't any tail." Then, after a moment's pause, "But look at those feet. They're positively human. Do you mean to say that this creature actually went up and opened our safe?"

"There are some things," Kildare answered quite calmly, "that I won't attempt to explain. But you can't deny certain facts." He stood up. "Monkeys have been trained to do some astounding things," he continued. "Have you ever thought what the result might be if a crossbreeding between a monkey and a human being were successful?"

"Good Lord," gasped Trask. "You mean this?"

"I'm not saying that it is," Kildare said, "but that's the only explanation I have for it."

"But surely," Trask argued, "there must have been someone with this beast, some keeper or something of the kind."

"Yes," Kildare nodded. "I'm going into that now."

The fog had cleared by this time, but Hazard's brain was in as deep a mist as any that had swirled through the streets of London that night. Suddenly, he stopped and caught his breath. Through the trees, his eyes had caught something, a horrible sight.

The trees stretched up along the fence just outside of the grounds, towering perhaps thirty feet in the air, and some of the branches overhung the iron spears. Dangling from the spikes of that fence was a blood-drenched figure. The figure of a Chinaman dressed in the costume of his people.

"Kildare!" Hazard cried. "For the love of heaven, look!"

He thought Kildare was smiling as he answered, "Yes, I see it. That's what I've been looking for. That completes the story and accounts for the blood in the bedroom."

He pointed directly across the lawn from the mangled figure to the house.

"Up there," he said, "is your father's bedroom, Trask. That man hanging on the fence was the keeper of the beast that killed your father. The little beast could get through because he was so small, but the keeper had to climb over to get into the enclosure. He probably pointed out the window of your father's bedroom and told the little beast what he was to do. From here it looks quite easy to climb up that tree from the outside and drop from that overhanging branch to the ground inside the fence. But as you can see, the limb broke and let the man down on the spikes. The little beast went to his master when he was in trouble, tried to help him. That's how he got smeared with blood. After he saw that it was useless, he left his master and went on to carry out his orders."

For a moment, Kildare stood looking in silence at the awful sight. Then he shrugged and moved toward it.

"Come on, Jerry," he said. "That's a nasty-looking mess up there. We'd better get it down."

Trask looked on with a mute, horrified expression as Kildare and Hazard climbed near the top of the fence and, after some effort, succeeded in lifting the body from the sharp prongs and lowering it to the ground.

Jerry Hazard took a long breath, bit his lip.

"What a rotten break!" he exploded. "We've got Wu Fang in jail, and we're cleaning up his agents. And yet, if that yellow devil is telling the truth, Mohra is back in Chinatown, held prisoner by some of these stinking rats of his."

Kildare frowned. He opened his mouth and was going to say something to Hazard, but at that moment, the sound of running feet reached them. Someone was rushing toward them from the door of the conservatory. It was the butler, running as fast as his stout legs would carry him.

"I say, sir, there's a telephone call for Mr. Kildare," he panted. "From Scotland Yard, sir. They say it's very important."

Kildare was off across the lawn at a fast pace, and Hazard was close behind him. The newspaperman was sure of the news the telephone call had carried. Scotland Yard had heard from the New York police. Mohra was safe—or gone. Mingled hope and desperation drove him to crowd Kildare to a faster pace. He waited breathlessly as the government man snatched the receiver and barked, "Hello," into the mouthpiece. Then he tensed as Kildare listened. He saw the government man's jaw muscles bulge, his whole body grow rigid. The knuckles of his left hand that clutched the receiver to his ears were white with the strain.

"Jove," he breathed. "Yes, I'll be right down."

Bang!

The receiver slammed on the hook, and Kildare spun around and headed for the front door of the mansion.

"Come on," he yelled. "You better go with us, Trask. Wu Fang has just escaped!"

CHAPTER 6
BEASTS OF DEATH

THE WHOLE world was reeling about Jerry Hazard as he darted after Kildare.

As they neared the entrance, the Trask gatekeeper stared in bewilderment at the three running men.

"Open the gate at once," Kildare ordered.

"Wait," Trask called out. "I'll get my car. It will be quicker."

Hazard and Kildare followed Trask toward the rear of the house, where a Rolls Phaeton stood at the open door of the garage. Trask leaped behind the wheel and started the motor as Kildare and Hazard piled in.

Kildare was mumbling to himself, "I was afraid of this very thing. Confound it, I had an idea that the Chief Inspector was too confident of his ability to hold Wu Fang."

"Did he give you any particulars?" Hazard asked.

"No, nothing," Kildare said. "He simply told me Wu Fang had escaped and that I had better get down as quickly as possible."

"But how in the name of heaven—" Hazard started to say.

"I haven't the slightest idea," Kildare cut in. "I'm very eager to find out myself how the yellow devil could get out of there. I hope we learn more about it when we reach headquarters."

The streets of London in the early hour of dawn were bare except for the usual smattering of market traffic. They had gone scarcely three blocks from the Trask mansion when Kildare, who was sitting in the back seat of the open car beside Hazard, jerked up straight. A cab was coming from the opposite direction.

Kildare called out a sharp command to Trask, but all too slowly the young banker heard him and clamped on the brakes of his powerful car.

Kildare jerked around in his seat, staring at the car that was passing them. Hazard's eyes were glued upon it, too. He saw a face in the rear window. It remained there for only a split second, but it made an indelible imprint on Hazard's brain.

"Nee-Sa!" Kildare rasped excitedly.

The government man was up in the car, snapping another order to Trask.

"Turn around as quickly as you can and follow that car," he cried.

Meantime, the cab had picked up speed and went tearing down the open street. In consternation, Trask was trying his best to get his long car turned around in the middle of the block. The Rolls was headed into the left curb, and Trask was about to back around.

Hazard was trying to follow the cab with his eyes. He saw it turn right at the next corner, traveling at a rapid rate of speed.

"Don't turn," Kildare shouted. "It will be easier to go straight ahead. Straighten up, Trask, and step on it. Hurry!"

Trask was doing his best. He spun the wheel laboriously and headed the great Rolls down the street again, the way they had been traveling.

"Turn left here," Kildare shouted as they reached the corner.

Looking back, Hazard could see that the cab had disappeared at the other end of the block, around that turn.

"Left again," Kildare snapped. "We're a block behind them. We've got to catch up. Nee-Sa is in that cab and heaven only knows who else."

The wheels of the Rolls skidded a little as they whirled around that next corner, again to the left. Far down that longer block, Hazard barely caught a glimpse of the rear end of the cab racing down the street past the corner. He made out a head in the cab but it was too far away to tell whether it was Nee-Sa.

"I see!" Trask cried out as the speedometer needle crept up to the 65 mark. Brakes squealed and the car lurched dizzily as they took the corner at a reckless pace.

Trask was staring down that main thoroughfare the way the cab had gone. But there was no cab in sight, nothing in the next block but a milk wagon on its morning rounds.

"They've gotten away from us," he groaned.

"That means they turned off on one of the side streets again," Kildare snapped. "Hurry! But be ready to swing either way at the next corner."

They raced on. Once more the tires squealed as they slowed at the cross-street intersection and stared in each direction. The cab was nowhere to be seen.

The Rolls had not stopped yet, but Kildare leaped for the door, flung it open and hit the sidewalk, running for a police signal box on the corner.

"Wait," he ordered. A bunch of keys jangled in his hand. He swung the door of the box open, grabbed the phone receiver, and clicked the hook frantically.

Hazard heard him say, "Kildare speaking. Have Limehouse completely surrounded. Give your men orders to search for cab number—"

Hazard didn't catch the rest of the conversation, for the Rolls had drifted past Kildare and stopped. A few moments later, the government man slammed the door of the iron box shut and ran back to the Rolls.

"On to headquarters," he ordered.

The sun was still far down behind the horizon when they drew up before Scotland Yard headquarters on the Thames embankment. They could see quite plainly out of doors, but Hazard noticed as they ran toward the entrance of the great building that it was almost totally dark inside.

TWO POLICE officers, typical English bobbies, stepped before them as they tried to enter. Hurriedly, Kildare gave his name and flashed his badge. The attitude of the police officers changed instantly.

"Yes, sir," one of them said. "We have had orders to be on the lookout for you. Come this way at once, Mr. Kildare."

The main room where they had been a few hours before was dark except for the sputtering dim lights shed by several candles. The police officer led them past the vacant desk of the Chief Inspector into a room at the side.

"Mr. Kildare, sir," he announced.

The Chief Inspector was pacing slowly across the room. Four still forms lay on the floor. The forms of four London police officers. The same surgeon who had administered first-aid to Hazard was making examinations. His face was a little white and considerably perplexed.

"What do you find?" Kildare demanded. "What's happened?"

The Chief Inspector looked haggard, but his voice was quite calm as he replied, "Wu Fang has escaped, sir."

"Yes, of course," Kildare said quickly. "You told me that over the phone. I mean what happened to these men? How did Wu Fang escape?"

Dangling from the spikes of that
fence was a blood-drenched figure.

The Inspector shook his head in a gesture of weary bewilderment.

"That's what I don't know," he admitted. "The whole thing is beastly uncanny."

"There was a girl in the case," Kildare ventured. "A Chinese girl about twelve years old. Am I right?"

The Chief Inspector's face reflected his amazement.

"But how did you guess it?" he asked incredulously.

"I didn't," Kildare told him. "I saw the Chinese girl, Nee-Sa, in a cab coming away from here not more than ten minutes ago. That's why I called. You sent out the orders that I suggested."

The Chief Inspector nodded again.

"Yes," he said, "the orders have been going out to the police of London ever since I got the news from you."

Kildare bent down beside the surgeon. "What's the cause of these deaths, Doctor?" he asked. He glanced from the police surgeon's face to the four bodies that had been stripped of their clothing.

The surgeon shook his head.

"I haven't decided yet," he said.

"Any marks on their bodies?"

"Not the slightest," the doctor replied. "That's what I'm looking up now. Naturally, from the way it happened, I'm assuming that they all met violent deaths."

"Have you made any tests for poison yet?" Kildare asked.

A look of indignation crossed the surgeon's face. "Well, really," he said, "one looks for traces of poison after one has found where the poison might have entered the body."

"Sometimes," Kildare said. "But with Wu Fang, perhaps you had better look for poison first and then try to find out how it got into the body."

The surgeon stiffened perceptibly.

"Perhaps you forget, Mr. Kildare," he said sharply, "that I have examined thousands of murdered humans during my service as police surgeon."

"I don't doubt that in the least," Kildare said calmly, "but apparently you have worked on very few cases where Wu Fang's victims were involved."

He turned abruptly to the Chief Inspector. "Now, sir, if you don't mind, would you give me the details? Tell me everything that happened. Don't leave out a thing. In the first place, you had three guards left about the double cell where Wu Fang was imprisoned, didn't you?"

"Yes," the Chief Inspector said, nodding. "I followed your suggestion, although I will admit I thought it a bit silly at first since no one has ever escaped from that cell before, even though it was unguarded."

"I can imagine," Kildare said, "that it would be a rather tough job for the average criminal. But go on, please. What happened after we left?"

"Well, sir, nothing happened for quite some time. Then a little girl came into my office. She said we were holding her father prisoner here."

"Her father!" Kildare exploded.

"Yes," the Chief Inspector nodded. "That's the way she put it."

Kildare's surprise subsided and he said, "All right. We'll let it go at that. And she wanted to see Wu Fang, of course?"

"Yes," answered the Inspector.

"Can you describe this girl to me so that we can be sure she was Nee-Sa?"

"Perfectly," the Chief said. "She was about twelve or thirteen years old, I should say. But it's hard to tell the exact age of these Orientals. She had the prettiest face for a Chinese girl that I have ever seen. It was very much like the face of an exquisite doll, and she wasn't so very much larger than a good-sized doll at that. She had been crying when she came in, and she was breathless from running. She said that if we would let her see her father for just a few minutes, that would be all she would ask."

The Inspector frowned at Kildare.

"You didn't tell me, Kildare," he said, "that Wu Fang had a daughter."

"I don't think he has," Kildare answered. "But at any rate, it made a good story for Nee-Sa. And this might interest you, if you happen to meet her again. Nee-Sa is one of the most fiendish little she-devils that ever was born, principally because she has such an innocent appearance. She's as clever as the very devil, Inspector, and she would stop at nothing to help Wu Fang. I'm sorry you didn't know about her beforehand."

"So am I," the Inspector said. "Well, to go on with the story, I couldn't see anything wrong in her request to see her father for a few minutes—at a distance, of course. I sent police officer Bigley in with her."

The Chief Inspector motioned to one of the corpses on the floor.

"THAT'S HIM there," he said. "I gave him orders to let her talk with the prisoner for ten minutes and then to bring her back to me. Of course, I specified that she was to stand outside in the corridor and talk through the bars. She seemed willing to do anything so long as she could see the yellow blighter she called her father.

"Ten minutes passed and they didn't come out. I was otherwise occupied and didn't notice the passing of time. Then it was fifteen minutes. I began to feel a bit anxious, so I got up from my desk and went in myself to see why my orders weren't being carried out.

"There in the corridor, I found these four bodies lying stretched out on the floor where they had fallen, stone dead. Three of them, of course, were the guards who were stationed outside the cell. The girl and the prisoner were nowhere to be found."

Hazard had been watching the Chief Inspector curiously as he talked, and now an exclamation suddenly forced itself from the newspaperman's lips.

"But how could they get out, Inspector?" he demanded. "Is there another door leading from the corridor?"

"No," the inspector said with a deep sigh. "That's what has me going about in circles, as you Americans say. There's no other way out except past my desk, and I'll swear to heaven that they didn't leave that way."

Hazard saw Kildare eyeing the Chief Inspector steadily. He was obviously deep in thought. He glanced about the room that was illuminated only by candles and several flashlights.

"When did these lights go off?" he asked.

"Oh, yes," the Chief Inspector said. "That's one detail I neglected to mention. About fifteen minutes had passed after the Chinese girl and Officer Bigley had gone back into the cell corridor. I began to wonder when they were going to return, when suddenly, all the lights in the building went out. I picked up my flash and went to see what was the matter. It was then that I saw these four dead."

"During that time," Kildare said, "the whole building was plunged into darkness?"

"That's correct," the Chief Inspector nodded.

"And now, one more question, Inspector, if you don't mind," Kildare said. He extended his hand toward the four bodies at his feet.

"As I recall when Wu Fang was locked up, one of these guards had the keys to his cell. Did you find them?"

Kildare didn't wait for a reply. He bent over the four naked corpses, and now he was speaking to the police surgeon.

"Any luck yet?" he asked.

The surgeon shook his head rather sullenly.

"None," he admitted.

"You don't mind if I make a little inspection of my own?" Kildare asked.

"Go as far as you like," the surgeon shrugged. "It's nothing to me."

Even before he had finished, Kildare was rolling the first body over on its stomach. He made a careful search of the flesh at the back of the neck, ran his fingers through the dead man's hair. Then he placed the body in its former position with the face staring up at the ceiling.

He examined the wrists and legs, all portions of the body that were most likely to be exposed to outward attack. He drew back the eyelids, spread the nostrils. The jaw dropped open easily as he pulled down on the chin, and he cast the ray of his flashlight inside the victim's mouth. He probed inside with the rubber end of a pencil.

"Hmm," he said, "that's interesting."

With that, he closed the mouth and moved on to the next corpse.

Hazard noticed that this time the examination of the neck and wrists and legs was shorter than the first; but the government man made a very careful inspection of the mouth.

He moved to the third body. This time he examined only the mouth of the victim.

The surgeon was looking on with sudden interest, but his voice was tinged with sarcasm as he asked, "Find something?" Kildare shrugged without turning.

"Don't know," he said shortly. "I can't be sure."

As he spoke, he was probing into the mouth of the third corpse as he had done with the first two. When he finished, he gave a short nod of satisfaction.

Now he was bending over the fourth body. The teeth gleamed in the rays of his flashlight.

Hazard saw Kildare frown and turn suddenly to the Inspector.

"Isn't this Bigley, the officer who took Nee-Sa back to see Wu Fang?" the government man asked.

"Yes," the Inspector nodded. "That's Bigley."

"Had he been eating something just before you sent him back to the cell?"

The Chief Inspector frowned in perplexity.

"Why, no," he said. "No, I'm sure of it. He had been there in my office for at least twenty minutes or a half-hour, and he hadn't been eating anything during that time. Why, what makes you ask?"

Without looking up, Kildare answered, "I just thought there might be a chance of it. There's a bit of raw flesh between his teeth."

"Raw flesh!" Those two words exploded in a chorus from the lips of every living man in the room.

"Yes," Kildare said calmly. "Get me a screwdriver. I can't open his jaws."

A screwdriver was procured and placed in the government man's hand.

"Thanks," he said. "I think I can make it by breaking the front teeth."

There came a crunching sound as Kildare wrenched the screwdriver handle.

"There," he said. Then he was probing in through the space

that he had made in the front of the mouth. His fingers clutched something, brought it out. It was a small piece of flesh that glistened in the light. Part of it was covered with skin.

Hazard couldn't see the thing very plainly from his angle, but he had seen enough. Cold chills raced up and down his spine.

Kildare was saying in a voice that sounded slightly hollow to Hazard, "You're lucky, Inspector, that only four of your men are dead. There are three of these things inside headquarters."

CHAPTER 7
THE GREEN DEATH

THE DEEP voice of the Chief Inspector boomed out in the room as he exclaimed, "Great Scott, man, what are you talking about? What is that thing you've got in your hand?"

As he spoke, he reached for the small, round bit of skin-covered flesh, but Kildare jerked his hand back.

"Just a minute," he said. "Be careful. One scratch of this deadly thing would mean instant death for you. Here, I'll hold it up so you can see it."

As he did so, Hazard saw the ghastly thing more clearly. It was the head of a snake not much more than a quarter of an inch thick and about an inch and a half long.

Carefully, Kildare pressed the sides of the jaws together, opened them wide enough so that the tiny fangs of the deadly reptile were plainly visible, gleaming red in the glow of the flashlight.

"But," said the surgeon who had been staring at the thing in wide-eyed amazement, "I still don't understand how that portion of an adder got into the mouth of Officer Bigley."

Kildare shrugged.

"It's very simple," he said. "Bigley apparently felt the snake trying to strike at his mouth and closed his jaws to keep it out. But he wasn't quick enough, for in doing so, he bit the snake in two—just as its fangs fastened in his tongue."

"Do you mean to say that these snakes were brought in by—" the Chief Inspector began.

Kildare nodded and smiled.

"I'm afraid you've guessed it," he said. "You made a fatal mistake, Inspector, when you permitted that girl to visit Wu Fang. I had no idea that anyone would be here to make a social call on that yellow devil, or I would have suggested that you let no one go near him."

"Yes," the Chief Inspector admitted gravely, "it seems that I used very poor judgment there. But this girl, why—she seemed so young, hardly more than a child. I never dreamed there was any danger in letting her see her father, particularly when there were a number of guards about his cell to keep her back."

"Excuse me, Mr. Kildare," the surgeon cut in, "but do I understand clearly that in all four cases, these officers were killed by an adder biting them in the tongue?"

"Yes," Kildare told him. "Here, I'll show you. There are two tiny marks on the tip of each tongue where they were struck."

He bent down and pointed to the tongue in the gaping mouth of the next victim.

"You see how the tongue is a slightly darker color than it should normally be?" he asked.

"Yes," the surgeon agreed. "I see that now."

"And here"—Kildare pointed with the tip of his lead pencil to two tiny marks on the tongue not more than an eighth of an inch apart—"is where the fangs went in."

"Have you ever seen a snake like it yourself?" the Inspector asked.

"No," Kildare said. "I don't have to. Except in a case like this, no one would be apt to see one of these things. I'll gamble that there isn't a wild creature of this species in existence."

"Then where on earth did this one come from?" the Chief demanded.

"This is one of the many beasts that Wu Fang and his agents have developed through a series of cross-breeding experiments," Kildare told him. "From its attack, this thing reminds me of a coral snake, and I wouldn't be surprised if it was partly derived from that species. They are one of the deadliest things that nature has ever conceived."

"But why," demanded the surgeon, "do they attack in the mouth of the victim?"

"They are trained to strike that way by the agents of Wu Fang," Kildare explained.

He held up the head again with the jaws open.

"Notice the length of the fangs," he said. "They are very tiny, scarcely more than a sixteenth of an inch long, and the mouth is small, too. That means that they must either chew their way into the flesh through the tough outside skin of a normal human being or else attack a place like the tongue, where the blood cells and nerve centers are very close to the surface. The tongue is so tender that these fangs merely have to scratch under the surface to send the poison into the victim's body and cause instant death."

"Great Scott!" the Chief Inspector groaned. "And you say there are three of them still loose in the rear cell block?"

"There must be unless they've escaped. A poisonous snake is quite apt to be cowardly just after it has struck a victim because it knows that with the emptying of its poison sacs, it is temporarily robbed of its power to kill."

"Yes, I know," the Chief nodded. "And that's the reason why we haven't seen these other three adders. They're hiding until their poison sacs are filled up again."

Kildare nodded.

"Right," he said. "And then they'll be out, killing once more. We've got to—"

Kildare stopped talking and seemed to freeze where he stood. Through the vaulted interior of the great Scotland Yard headquarters, an awful cry rang out.

Kildare was racing out the door, shining his flashlight beam ahead of him. He snatched the nightstick from the hands of one of the bobbies as he passed.

THEY CHARGED into the main headquarters office, where flickering candles sent weird, frantic beams across the room, making the huge moving shadows seem like phantoms flitting ahead of them.

The cry came again and again. A scream of mortal anguish and pain.

"Help! Help! A snake! It's on me! It—"

"Bring the keys to these cells," Kildare shouted to the Inspector. "We haven't got a second to lose. These prisoners are trapped like rats."

As they broke into the corridor that was flanked on each side by cells, Kildare shouted encouragement to the screaming prisoner.

The tiny beast was at the doomed prisoner's mouth.

"We're coming! Fight it off! Don't let it get near your mouth."

Then the man's desperate screams were suddenly choked off as though paralysis had suddenly seized his vocal cords.

Except for the faint gray light of dawn that filtered dimly through the high, narrow windows, Kildare's flashlight was the only illumination in the corridor.

They were running straight for the cell where the cry had come from. Hazard was there beside Kildare, staring into the cell. The light shadowed the bars, fan-shaped across the floor, and in these stripes, a figure lay slumped, mouth open and muscles still twitching in the last throes of death.

Hazard's bulging eyes saw something else in there, a tiny object moving rapidly across the floor away from the face of the dead man. It was a snake, scarcely more than four inches long, with a head exactly like the one Kildare had taken from the mouth of officer Bigley.

Now the tiny, deadly reptile was making his way to the cell next on the left as fast as he could wriggle. The prisoner in that cell was staring at it, standing in the middle of his cage, transfixed with fear.

"Don't—don't let him get me!" he cried frantically. "For the love of heaven, save me! Save me!"

Kildare was yelling, "Quick! The keys! We've got to get into this next cell."

Then, to the prisoner he cried, "Stamp the snake to death when it comes through the bars. It can't hurt you unless it bites you in the mouth."

But even then, the prisoner's mouth was open as he stared

in stupefied horror. His tongue seemed to be stuck in his throat. He tried to speak, but no words would come.

At the partition between the cells, the tiny reptile of death started up one of the iron bars, wriggling with amazing speed up toward the top.

Kildare stuck his arm between two bars near the partition, tried with all his might to reach the beast with his nightstick and knock it down. He missed it by the space of a few inches.

He cried again to the prisoner, "Knock it down, I tell you. Don't be afraid to use your hands!"

There was a jangle of keys; the Chief Inspector was struggling frantically to unlock the cell.

The snake had reached the top of the cage and was going across to a point above the panic-stricken man's head. It seemed almost as though the little creature had hypnotic powers over his victim.

"Get out from under it, you fool!" Kildare yelled. "Haven't you got any control over your legs at all?"

At the same time, Hazard, Trask, and the Scotland Yard inspectors were fairly screaming advice to the doomed prisoner. Then a key clicked in the lock and the bolt shot back. Kildare hurled the heavy door back and leaped in.

Swish!

Hazard saw Kildare strike out with his nightstick, heard a sharp smack as it collided with the little adder. A spurt of blood spattered on the newspaperman's face.

The flashlight beam dropped to the floor. Kildare's club swished through the air twice, made resounding thuds as it landed on the hard paving. Then he bent over, scooped the mangled body of the snake on the end of the stick. He turned to the Chief Inspector.

"Have you any objections to my running the show a little while longer?" he asked.

"No, indeed," came the answer. "This is something a bit out of my line."

"Good," Kildare said. He snapped an order to the other inspectors who were gathered about the corridor. "Take your positions with flashlights the length of the cell block. I want as much light as you can possibly get."

The Chief Inspector had already locked the door to the cell that Kildare and Hazard had just left. The prisoner had dropped down on his bunk, trembling with fright.

"NOW, THEN," Kildare said, raising his voice and addressing the other prisoners. "One man has been killed. We want to save the rest of you if we can. We're going to give you as much light as possible."

As the flashlight beams sprayed about the darkness, Hazard could see the prisoners through the bars, gingerly shaking out their bed clothing, staring warily up over their heads.

Turning to the Chief Inspector, Kildare said, "Be ready with that bunch of keys."

Two, three minutes of tense waiting. Then a cry came from the far end of the corridor.

"Get him! Get him! He's above me. He's going to—"

Kildare and Hazard and the Chief Inspector were on a dead run toward that cell from where the cry came.

This prisoner was small and wiry and showed no traces of the paralyzing fear that had gripped the other. They saw him step back as the dully-gleaming snake dropped from the ceiling.

As it struck the floor, the Inspector flung open the barred door and Kildare lunged in with his nightstick upraised. But the prisoner reached the snake first and stood angrily stamping the reptile to a pulp. But even then, the head continued to writhe and strike and the deadly jaws were open and gnashing.

Wham!

Kildare struck at that vicious head and crushed it. He turned to the prisoner, who was clutching his arm. He was a small, gray-haired man with stooped shoulders. As he came over from the end of the cell where Kildare had thrown him, they could see that he limped slightly. His voice rasped when he spoke, but it was pitifully pleading.

"I ain't of much account guv'nor," he said, "but I'm a human being, and I ain't so bad as some folks might think I am. Beggin' your pardon, sir, I want to tell you what a brave man you are and how thankful I am to you. Maybe I won't never be able to do nothing for you, but I get out of here tomorrow, the king and queen willin', God bless 'em. I'll be looking after any help I can give you. I know about the bloomin' yellow blighter that just escaped, and I hope you catch him, sir, if I may say so."

"Thanks, old man, for wishing me luck in catching Wu Fang," Kildare said as he placed a hand on the gray-haired convict's shoulder. "And lots of luck to you. You'll find it pretty tough to go straight when you first get out, but it's the only way."

"Yes, sir," the prisoner agreed, "and I'm the man what knows that."

As Kildare turned to go, the man called after him, "My name is John Doakes, and anytime you need me, don't be afraid to call on me."

"Mr. Kildare," the Chief Inspector said, as they entered the main office, "I congratulate you on your work tonight. I assume all blame for the escape of Wu Fang. I know that you have been at least partially dismissed from the bureau of investigation. Scotland Yard would be highly honored to have you in their service."

Kildare smiled his pleasure.

"That's mighty nice of you, Inspector," he said, "but I'm afraid it wouldn't fit in with my scheme of things—at least not until Wu Fang is finished."

"I appreciate your point of view," the Chief said, "and of course, we all respect you for it, but"—here the Inspector returned Kildare's smile—"blast it all, you haven't told me how Wu Fang and the girl escaped."

Kildare laughed.

"I'M SORRY, Inspector," he said. "I forgot all about that point. I thought perhaps you would have it figured out by this time. They passed you somewhere in the corridor."

"But they couldn't have," the Chief said, frowning. "I had a flashlight with me. I'm sure there was no one in the corridor besides me."

"Oh, I don't mean exactly that they brushed by you," Kildare said, still smiling. "Remember, the keys that one of the guards had disappeared and they haven't been found yet. Of course, I'm not a mind reader and I didn't actually see it happen, but it would be a simple matter for them to get out of the double cell after Nee-Sa killed the guards and someone cut the light wires. All they would have to do then would be to come down the corridor in the darkness, find an empty cell, unlock it, and wait in it until you passed. After that, all they had to do was walk on through the darkness out the front door."

The Chief looked perplexed for a moment. Then he turned to his desk and smiled sheepishly.

"Oh, by the way," he said, "I got an answer to your cablegram, Mr. Hazard. It came in just before all this excitement occurred."

He picked up an envelope from the table and handed it to Hazard. The newspaperman took the missive with trembling fingers and tore it open. A great lump rose in his throat as he read the contents:

POLICE GUARDS HAVE NOT SEEN MOHRA IN FOUR DAYS.

The cablegram was signed by a deputy inspector of the New York police.

The blood surged through Hazard's brain, pounded at his temples.

"It's true," he groaned. "Wu Fang was telling the truth. They've got her."

He felt Kildare's hand on his shoulder, heard him say, "Take it easy, Jerry. There's something funny here."

The telephone bell jangled, and the Chief Inspector picked up the instrument.

"I'm washed up here," Hazard told Kildare through clenched teeth. "I'm going back to New York, and I'm going to find Mohra if I have to turn the whole of Chinatown upside-down."

Suddenly the Chief Inspector's voice rang out in a low command.

"Get on that other phone," he ordered Kildare as he pointed to another instrument on his desk. Then into the mouthpiece of his phone, he said, "Righto. Will you repeat that last, please?"

Kildare was on the other phone, tense, listening.

Hazard had turned and was going toward the door. He stopped suddenly as he heard the Inspector breathe, "Great Scott!" Kildare was pressing the receiver close to his ear, straining to catch every word. There came a sigh, and both receivers clicked on their hooks.

"Did you ever hear anything like it?" the Chief asked. "The entire population of Glenderm is dead—wiped out. Strange, those bodies must have been lying there for days. They're green with rot."

"No," Kildare contradicted. "Give me a map, quick! Show me where Glenderm is."

The room, which had been fairly quiet a few moments before, now teemed with tense anxiety.

"I say," Trask exploded. "Glenderm! Why, that's—" He stopped short, bit his lip.

Hazard saw Kildare raise his eyes and shoot a keen glance

at young Trask. Then he returned to his study of the map. The Chief Inspector glanced at his watch hurriedly.

"Glenderm is not more than an hour and a half from here by express," he said, "and I believe there's a train leaving for there in about five or ten minutes."

He straightened, faced Kildare.

"I say," he exploded suddenly. "It's Wu Fang. He's been out just about long enough to get up there by the last train. But— the green rot." He shook his head. "No, that couldn't be it. It takes days for mold like that to form on bodies."

"No," Kildare said slowly, "it's not mold. I'm sure of it. It's"— he hesitated for a perceptible moment—"the green death."

CHAPTER 8
THE VILLAGE OF DOOM

AS THE express train roared through the English countryside at a speed of almost ninety miles an hour, Hazard tried to compose himself. Every minute that he traveled on this train was taking him farther away from Mohra.

Now and then he glanced at the number one government man, but always Kildare was in the same position, slumped well down in his seat, long legs crossed, and a thin cigar in his mouth as he stared reflectively out the window.

At length, the train drew into the station of the city nearest to Glenderm, and they were transferred to a slower train on a branch of the main railroad. Not long afterward, they drew up to the little station of Glenderm.

At first glance, the little village snuggled on the edge of the moors looked very peaceful. Beyond, they could see, as they left the train, the heather-dotted moors stretching in tumbled wastes as far as the eye could travel.

Kildare, Hazard, the Chief Inspector, and several of the Scotland Yard men were the only ones to leave the train at that station. Trask had been left in London under heavy guard.

The only person visible was a police officer from a nearby city. He saluted the Chief and motioned toward the station interior.

"Here's one victim you can see," he announced.

Hazard saw a ghastly sight inside the ticket office of the little station. The body of a man lay stretched on the floor. His hands, face, neck—every part of his body that was not covered by his clothing—was a horrible green color.

Kildare bent down instantly and began inspecting the dead man's body while the Chief Inspector examined it from the other side. Hazard saw the Chief rub his finger across the cheek and neck of the dead station agent.

"This isn't mold," he said, glancing up at the police officer. "Great Scott, man, the very skin itself is green."

"Yes," the officer nodded, "we found that out as soon as we reached here."

Kildare got up.

"How did you learn about this in the first place?" he demanded.

"Someone called from here," the officer responded.

"But I say," the Chief Inspector cried, "you mean some inhabitant of the village is alive to tell about this?"

"No, sir. As a matter of fact, the man who notified us is almost crazy and he wasn't a villager either. I'll tell you how it happened, sir. It's a bit of a strange story. We received a call this morning at headquarters. You see, I'm on the police force at Pitkin. That's the city where you changed trains, I believe."

Kildare and the Chief Inspector nodded.

"Well, you see, sir, this man called us this morning. He was very excited, and at first we couldn't make out what he was talking about. Finally we made out that he was a farmer from up above Glenderm. Just after daybreak, when he brought his butter and eggs to town, he found the body of one of his customers lying in the street. It was green, just like this one, sir."

The officer pointed to the dead station agent.

"The farmer told us he had hurried to the main street to notify the constable, but there he found bodies lying all over the street. There were men, women and children—and even a horse—lyin' dead in the gutter there on the main street. Most of the town, though, was still asleep. People were dead and rotten green in their beds. Every corpse was the same color. The farmer used the constable's telephone to call Pitkin."

The Chief Inspector nodded. "And as soon as you received his message you called us at Scotland Yard without waiting to come up and make an investigation?"

"That's right, sir. You see, we figured it was something quite out of the ordinary, and that we should let you know about it."

Men, women and children lay dead in the streets.

"Yes," Kildare cut in, "that's quite obvious. And what have you found since you've been here?"

"The only living soul we found was the farmer. One of our officers took him back to Pitkin, sir. He seemed to be losing his mind."

"You mean," the Chief Inspector demanded, "that this farmer is going mad?"

"Yes, sir," the officer nodded. "We were afraid he might commit suicide. You can imagine, sir, that it must have been a horrible experience for him."

"Yes," Kildare agreed, "I haven't any doubt of it. Have you made a complete check of the people of the town since you came?"

The officer nodded affirmatively.

"Three hundred ninety-six, all of them dead and turned green," he said, "when we made the last count, sir."

"Let's have a look at the rest of him," Kildare suggested.

His fingers became immediately busy undoing the clothing and stripping it off the dead man. Hazard was helping him while the Chief Inspector looked on.

There was no mark on the body, no sign of any kind that would tell how he met his death. Nothing, that is, except the weird, green color of the skin. It was not a clear green, like the color of grass, but rather it looked as though mustard had been mixed with it, giving an appearance of sodden decay, as though the body would fall apart at the least touch.

"He hasn't been dead very long," Kildare commented as he made a hasty examination.

"That's what I guessed," the Chief Inspector agreed. "Certainly not long enough for that green color to come from any formation of mold on his body."

Kildare finished his inspection in silence. Then he stood up and shrugged.

"It's one on me," he said.

The Chief Inspector's face fell.

"I'M SORRY to hear that," he said. "I was hoping from what you said before we left Scotland Yard that you had some idea of the method that was used to inflict this death."

Kildare glanced at him quickly.

"Did I say something to that effect?" he asked.

"You said," the Inspector reminded him, "that it wasn't mold that caused these bodies to turn green; that it was the 'green death.' Do you know anything about a 'green death' that might affect people in this manner?"

"No," Kildare said, shaking his head. "But it is a green death. We can't deny that." He started for the door. "Let's go take a look at the other poor devils."

"They're all the same," the Pitkin officer assured him.

"No doubt," Kildare allowed, "but let's have a look just the same."

As they entered the main street of the village, a horrible sight met their eyes. Perhaps a dozen bodies cluttered the gutter, while the green rotted-looking carcass of a horse lay dead across the rude cobblestones. Other officers from Pitkin were taking bodies from the houses.

The officer turned to the Chief Inspector.

"You see, sir, our men from Pitkin have been digging graves over back of the church. We're afraid that this may be some awful and contagious disease."

"That was a very wise move," the Chief Inspector said. "I think it would be well to dispose of the bodies as quickly as possible. We don't know what it is that has killed them yet—do we, Kildare?"

The government man shook his head.

"No," he said, "but I believe it would be best, Inspector, if you made a formal announcement to the effect that these mass deaths have not been caused by disease."

"Do you think it would be wise if I permitted the newspapers to print the suspicion that Wu Fang probably is responsible for all this?" the Chief demanded.

"No, I don't believe I would say anything about him either," Kildare advised. "It isn't going to help any to have the entire population of the British Isles half-mad with fear."

Hours passed, and still the work of searching and inspection went on. Kildare said little except to ask a question now and then.

"I can't help thinking," the Chief Inspector said presently, "that Wu Fang is behind this. I'm quite sure that he had time, though, to get up here after his escape."

"It's possible," Kildare admitted. "Barely possible. That's one of the things I'm trying to learn, what time these deaths occurred."

As he walked behind Kildare, Hazard suddenly saw that the government man had stopped and was staring at one of the trees in the street. The Chief Inspector had gone on a little distance ahead.

"This is a neat little town, Jerry," Kildare said. "The gardens are in good condition, the lawns are mowed—in fact, the whole place has the appearance of being nicely kept up. But the trees—"

Hazard saw immediately what he meant, for beneath the trees were broken branches and even fresh leaves.

"What does that remind you of?" Kildare asked softly.

Hazard hesitated.

"Why—why, it looks very much as though they've had a heavy wind through here," he said.

"Exactly," Kildare nodded. "In London, a hundred and forty or fifty miles away, they had a heavy fog. Here, they apparently had a heavy wind."

Without making any reference to the trees, Kildare casually asked one of the Pitkin officers, "How was the weather last night and this morning, do you remember?"

"Yes, sir," the officer nodded. "I was on night duty, sir. I should say that altogether it was a nice calm evening."

"Thanks," Kildare nodded. He sought out the officer they had met in the mayor's house, the one who had been raised in Glenderm.

"How long ago did you move away from Glenderm, Officer?" he asked.

"It was about six years ago," the officer replied.

"You knew everyone here pretty well, didn't you?" Kildare queried.

"Yes," the officer nodded. "There wasn't a bloomin' soul in or about Glenderm that I didn't know."

Suddenly Kildare brightened as though a thought had come to him.

"Oh, by the way," he said, "I met a man recently in London whom I think has spent quite a bit of time up here on the moors near Glenderm. Comes up for a bit of hunting during his vacations. Let me see, his name is—" Kildare pretended to be searching his mind for the name. "Trask. Yes, that's it. I believe he has a hunting lodge up here somewhere."

The officer nodded at once.

"YES, SIR," he said. "Mr. Trask, the great London banker. He's a very fine man, sir. My father helped build his lodge. It's up on the moors about four miles from here, sir."

Kildare turned with apparent uncertainty.

"Let's see, the hunting lodge would be—"

The police officer pointed quickly up a side street and off to the north.

"Up that way, sir," he said. "You take this side street, and it runs into a dirt road that's in fair condition and winds about the moors. It ends, after about four miles, at Mr. Trask's hunting lodge."

"Thanks," Kildare said. "I was just wondering where it might be. You see, when I met young Trask recently, he invited me to come up for some shooting when the season opens."

They walked on down the street, stepping over bodies and around trucks that were hauling the dead away toward the freshly-dug graves. It was getting quite late in the afternoon.

"I don't get you at all, Kildare," Hazard said when no one could overhear them. "Trask didn't invite you up to his hunting lodge, did he?"

"No." Kildare smiled. "As a matter of fact, he didn't even tell me openly that he had one."

"Then what—" Hazard began.

"Sssh!" Kildare cut in. "Here comes the Chief Inspector. I don't want him to know."

A moment later, the Chief Inspector joined them.

"I say," he admitted, "it's the most baffling thing I've ever seen in my life. I can't make head nor tail out of it."

They went on together from house to house through the afternoon. Now and then Kildare seemed to be trying to break away from the Chief Inspector, but whenever he suggested that he and Hazard go in one direction to look into matters further on, the Scotland Yard man followed.

The day was hot and sultry, and the sun had been burning down intensely on the little village in the valley below the moors. Now great clouds towered in the west, and it grew dark. Thunderheads warned of approaching storms.

At length, Kildare turned to the Chief Inspector and said, "I believe we had better get started back for London."

The Inspector looked at him quickly.

"Why?" he asked.

"Because," the government man answered, "this job here is done. If Wu Fang is behind this mass killing, it was obviously a trial of a death machine. A trial that was horribly successful. You can imagine where he will strike next."

"Good heavens!" the Inspector cried. "You don't mean London?"

"That's exactly the idea," Kildare said. "My advice to you would be to round up your men as quickly as possible and take the next train back."

"And you'll go along with us?" the Chief asked.

"You'll probably see us on the train," Kildare told him.

"Righto," he said. "I'll be looking for you."

Kildare walked leisurely up the street, and Hazard kept close beside him. He glanced at the ominous, threatening storm clouds overhead.

"I'm afraid we're in for it, Jerry," he said. "Feel as though you could stand a good wetting?"

"A good wetting!" Hazard repeated. "But look here. We'll be on the train or at least in the station by the time that storm breaks."

Kildare smiled in the dim twilight. "We're not taking the train, Jerry."

Suddenly, the truth dawned on the newspaperman.

"You mean," he demanded, "that you're going up to that hunting lodge?"

Kildare nodded.

"But I don't understand at all," Hazard persisted. "How—"

"Sssh!" Kildare admonished. "Here's one of those Pitkin policemen."

He stopped and spoke to the officer.

"We're trying to round up the Scotland Yard men who came

with us," he told him. "If you see anything of them, tell them they're wanted at the station at once."

"Yes, sir." The policeman nodded and moved on.

The two men walked for perhaps a half block down that side street. Hazard's head was swimming with uncertainty. This trip into the moors was taking him still farther away from Mohra.

"Look here, Kildare, I'm not—"

"I know what you're thinking," Kildare interrupted with a smile. "But let me assure you that you could do nothing to help Mohra. Nothing, do you understand? In the first place, there's something funny about her disappearance four days ago. Remember that. It was only last night that Wu Fang said he had received word from his agents in New York that Mohra had been captured. Now you hear that her guards haven't seen her for four days. Don't you see?"

By now they were striding rapidly along a dirt road that led from the village. It took them over a little knoll and down into a valley on the other side. The town was completely hidden from view now.

Hazard heard Kildare take a long breath.

"There," he said, "that's better. I was afraid they would see us going this way, but I don't think they suspect."

As they left the town, darkness was descending abruptly. Darkness made all the more gruesome by the rumble of thunder from behind.

"This experience should be interesting," Hazard said. "I've read about thunderstorms on the moors, but I never was in one."

As though to punctuate his words, a terrific crash of thunder sounded from behind.

Bam!

It seemed to strike at their very heels. The air about them was vibrant with electricity. At the same time, a blinding flash of lightning illuminated the great heather wastes about them with a weird light quite unlike any Hazard had ever seen. Somehow he sensed that out there beyond them was something mysterious, ghastly and threatening.

Kildare had stopped and was staring out across the stretches of moorlands.

"Jove," he breathed. "Look, Hazard!" He was pointing straight ahead of them. "Look out there across that next moor!"

CHAPTER 9
DEATH'S CRADLE

HAZARD STARED with bulging eyes. The lightning rippled again, the thunder crashed, then all was still. As Kildare moved ahead again, Hazard spoke. His voice was hushed and shaken.

"There's something uncanny out here on the moors. Kildare, you know a lot you're not telling. What is it?"

Kildare's voice came to him, reassuringly calm.

"We're all right, Jerry," he said, "so long as another experiment isn't made while we're going those four miles."

"Experiment?" Hazard demanded.

"Yes," Kildare said. "There's some terrific force been at work through here. You saw the same thing I did in that flash of lightning. How far would you say we've gone since we left Glenderm?"

Hazard thought it was perhaps a mile.

"All right then, we're within three miles of the hunting lodge. Here."

He picked up a piece of heather and held it up before the light. The end where it fastened to the roots was twisted and torn.

"You see," Kildare said, "whatever this powerful agent was that swept across the moors, it mowed down the heather and every living thing in its path."

"Yes," Hazard said, "and we'll see more of it as we go on, if the lightning continues to flash."

"They say," Kildare remarked as they strode on, "that the moors at night are apt to get you. I guess that's true, all right. The thing that struck me so forcibly, on seeing this great swath of heather torn down and strewn about, was the fact that I could fairly feel some terrific force that had swept through here like a phantom flood. And then look—" He held the branch of heather that he still carried before his flashlight. "Notice how the bark and leaves are stripped clean from the branch."

Blam!

As they strode on hurriedly, the first drops of rain began to fall, and a few moments later, it was coming down in torrents.

But Jerry Hazard took little notice of it. His mind was tortured by thoughts far more troublesome than a mere thunderstorm. He burst out, "Kildare, for the love of heaven, tell me why you're rushing off across these wastes to Trask's hunting lodge. Is Wu Fang here."

"No," Kildare breathed, "I hope not. That's why I'm hurrying."

"I suppose," Hazard said a trifle bitterly, "you're having a lot of fun keeping your reason to yourself. If you won't answer that question, then tell me why you ran away from the Scotland Yard men. Why didn't you want them to know that you were coming out here? Why don't you think that Wu Fang murdered those people in the village?"

"I'll answer the last question first," Kildare said. "In the first place, those people weren't murdered."

"Weren't murdered!" Hazard exploded.

"No," Kildare said. "Their deaths were accidental, and of course, being accidental, Wu Fang didn't do it. That yellow devil never does anything by mistake. In fact, Jerry, he couldn't have done it."

"I don't see why," Hazard argued. "You admitted yourself that he had time to get up here after his escape from prison."

"Well, Jerry, I must confess that I was slightly off in my calculations. A thorough examination showed that the deaths occurred within five or ten minutes of six o'clock. Dawn breaks at that hour, this time of the year, and if you remember, Wu Fang escaped just at dawn."

Kildare continued, "You know, Jerry, I'm well acquainted with towns like Glenderm. The population is mostly made up of retired farmers who have come to live in town. All the early rising habits of their farming days stay with them, and dawn finds most of the town up and about. The very fact that most of the bodies were still in bed convinces me that the holocaust could not have struck the town later than six or six-fifteen.

"Those ten or twelve bodies that were in the street," the government man went on, "were those of the real early birds of the town. You see, it was impossible for Wu Fang to have arrived here in time to have committed this deed."

"I suppose it was," Hazard admitted, "But his agents—"

"His agents," Kildare corrected, "would have had to discover the death apparatus almost at the same time that Wu Fang was trying the other one out on you. That doesn't sound plausible, because if his agents had discovered the new machine, they would have notified Wu Fang immediately, before they did anything about it."

"But why were you trying to keep the Scotland Yard men in the dark?" Hazard repeated.

"I'll have to explain that by telling you something else first," Kildare answered. "I'll tell you why I'm going to Trask's hunting lodge. You remember when we were questioning Trask and I asked him where the inventor was? I caught him a little off guard. Do you recall his answer?"

"No," Hazard said. "I remember he started to say something and then stopped."

"**HE SAID**," Kildare told him, " 'He's at our—'That was all, but it was enough because it gave me the idea that the inventor was at some place owned by the Trasks. And then at Scotland Yard, when the news came over the phone concerning the mass deaths at Glenderm, Trask blurted out, 'I say, that's near our—' and again he stopped."

"Good Lord!" Hazard breathed. "You mean the inventor of this death ray, or whatever it is, is up here at the hunting lodge?"

"I never was surer of anything in my life," Kildare admitted.

"But why don't you want Scotland Yard to know?" Hazard asked for the third time.

"I'm coming to that," Kildare said, striding on at a faster gait through the storm. "I'm afraid that they would mess things up rather badly. If Wu Fang isn't responsible for the killing of these people, then someone else is. And if I'm right in believing that the inventor of this death machine is hiding at the Trask hunting lodge while he's working on this machine, then my guess is that he's the guilty person."

A feeling of horror suddenly gripped Hazard as he demanded, "You mean that he deliberately murdered those people to try out his machine?"

"No," Kildare said patiently. "Remember, a few minutes ago I told you that these deaths were caused accidentally. Let's hurry on."

They had been striding on in the rain for nearly an hour since they had left Glenderm. They topped another knoll and started down the other side.

Blam!

With a roar and a crash, another bolt rent the heavens and spread its weird light across the moor. Hazard's eyes popped. In a little depression at the bottom of the hill, he saw a building, large and rambling, and surrounded by trees that had obviously been imported from some foreign region.

Out of the corner of his eye, Hazard saw Kildare staring at

The blow exploded full in Hazard's face.

something else. Something near the side of the road. Before he could catch sight of it, the darkness had hemmed them in once more.

Hazard heard Kildare muttering, "I guessed something like that. I think that answers the question."

Hazard followed Kildare to the side of the road. The government man took out his pocket light and flashed it on. There beside the road, about a thousand feet from the house, a stake had been driven into the ground. To the stake was tied a horse, a gaunt, old animal whose ribs were plainly visible under his skin. He was sprawled on the ground, dead.

Kildare bent over the animal's body, ran his hand over the hair, holding his light close.

"Look, Jerry," he said in a voice that was almost triumphant. "Green! The horse's skin is green!"

The newspaperman was staring in amazement.

Kildare snapped off the light, and they hurried on.

"Come on," the government man cried, starting toward the house again. "Now I'm positive I'm right."

A few moments later, they were at a gate that surrounded an ample lawn. The house was totally dark. From somewhere behind the house, the bellowing bark of a great dog came to them, echoing weirdly across the moors.

Blam!

Another terrific clap of thunder followed closely on the heels of a blinding flash of lightning, as Kildare pushed through the gate. Hazard saw that the government man held his gun in his hand, snatched his own out of his pocket. The bold bark of the dog ended in a whine of fear.

When they reached the front door, Hazard knocked.

"We're friends of Gerald Trask," he called out. "Let us in."

They waited for a short time, but no sound came from within.

Again Kildare knocked and called out. Then from behind the heavy front door came sounds of shuffling footsteps. A bolt shot back, and the door opened a little way. They could just see the vague outline of a face peering out at them over the beam of a flashlight that was aimed directly into their faces. Hazard could tell from the man's height that he was taller than Kildare.

"This is a private hunting lodge," a deep, rasping voice said. "I'm giving you fair warning. You'd better get out before it's—"

The man stopped talking as his gaze shifted to the two guns. Then Kildare was moving swiftly. He whirled and charged the partly open door. Hazard went to his friend's aid, his shoulder hitting the door with a bang.

Hazard darted through the opening after Kildare. The government man was trying to say something.

"We're friends of Trask," he said. "We came to—"

Something flashed before the light that had been shining into Hazard's face, and he felt the blow smack full on his jaw. His head reeled, stars danced, and he was hurling backward into a black void.

CHAPTER 10
YELLOW FACES

JERRY HAZARD wasn't out long. As he opened his eyes, he was aware of a buzz of conversation and of lights above him. Things stopped spinning, and Kildare bent over him.

"Come on, Jerry, snap out of it," he said. "You're OK."

As Kildare helped him to his feet, Hazard glanced at the two figures before him. One was the big, powerful brute of a man who had opened the door. His nose was flattened and his ears were scarred.

"I'm glad you're all right," the smaller man said with a grin. "I'm sorry that I hit you so hard."

Kildare introduced Hazard to the man who had knocked him out. "This is Mr. Kent, the inventor of the death machine."

Hazard was a little taken aback as he acknowledged the introduction. Somehow, he hadn't expected the inventor to be this kind of a man. He was a strong, healthy-looking individual about the same build as Hazard. The description "English sportsman" fitted him to a T, Hazard decided.

"This is Bing O'Flynn," Kent said, turning to the big fellow beside him. "He's my chief cook and bottle washer, as well as bodyguard. He was my trainer when I used to go in for boxing."

Jerry Hazard stared hard at the Englishman. He was sure he recognized him now.

"You mean," he demanded, "that you're Jack Kent, amateur champion of the London A.C.?"

Kent grinned. "Righto," he said. "It was good sport while it lasted, but then I became interested in science and invention."

Hazard looked from Kent to Kildare and back to Kent again.

"You admit, then, that you're the inventor of this death machine?" he asked.

Kent merely smiled; Kildare laughed heartily.

"You haven't been out very long, Jerry," the government man said. "Not long enough for either of us to go into details to any extent."

Kildare glanced significantly about the place, and Hazard

saw that they were in a large living room with a great fireplace at one end.

"Suppose we sit down and talk this thing over," Kildare suggested.

"Righto," the English sportsman-inventor agreed. He turned to the big fellow and asked, "Bing, how about a fire? These men are soaked to the skin."

"Right you are." Bing O'Flynn grinned and trotted off for some wood.

While they seated themselves about the fireplace, the former boxing trainer kindled a fire. Outside, the storm raged on, but before the flames of that welcome blaze, some of the recent horrors were forgotten for the moment.

Kildare and Hazard took off part of their wet clothes, and Bing draped them before the fire to dry. Kildare caught Kent's eye and nodded significantly to the bodyguard.

"I'm wondering," he said in a low voice, "if we shouldn't talk some of these things over alone."

Kent smiled reassuringly.

"Bing knows all that goes on here," he said. "He can be trusted absolutely. Please go ahead."

Bing had left the room while they were talking. He returned now with two bathrobes over his arm. Hazard and Kildare put them on, and the trainer hung their underclothing up to dry before the fire.

"Very well," Kildare said, "let's see how good a clairvoyant I am. You are up here in the Trask hunting lodge, perfecting a certain new type of death machine."

119

Kildare was eyeing the inventor keenly, but Kent remained silent.

"Your first machine didn't prove so satisfactory," Kildare continued. "It was some sort of an elaboration on an X-ray machine, and although it would kill, it was not effective at any great distance."

Kent nodded. "You're doing very well so far."

"You borrowed money from Bertrand Trask and his son, Gerald, so that you could carry on your work to develop a device that would kill at a fairly long range. You intended, of course, to sell this invention, when completed, to the British government for use in time of war. You left the plans of your first invention with the Trasks as security."

"That checks very well," Kent admitted.

KILDARE CONTINUED, "Since the Trasks had no particular use for the hunting lodge at this time, they suggested that you come up here, where you could work on your invention. Last night or early this morning, you finally completed your machine of death. You had to have something on which to try it out, so you got hold of an old horse that should have been shot long ago and tied him to a stake about a thousand feet from the house. Then you turned your death machine on him for a length of time.

"When you completed your experiment, you walked up the hill and inspected the animal. I believe, if you looked closely enough, you saw that the horse's skin had turned green under the hair. This, I assume, was a result that you didn't quite expect."

Kildare paused. Kent was leaning forward excitedly in his chair.

"God," he said, "that's perfect! How in the world did you ever guess it?"

"It wasn't exactly a guess," Kildare said. "Certain circumstances that have happened in the last twenty-four hours all pointed to this fact."

He told Kent of his learning that Trask was financing a mysterious invention and of the sensational developments of the last few days. He finally spoke of the news that Scotland Yard received concerning the strange deaths in Glenderm.

When he reached that point, Kent's face was working convulsively.

"Do you mean that my ray killed someone besides the old horse?"

Kildare broke the news to him as gently as he could.

"Listen, Kent," he said, "you will have to try and take this as philosophically as possible. I'm afraid it's going to be an awful blow to you. It proves that your invention is a complete success, but it also means that you have innocent blood on your hands."

Kent leaped up from his chair. There was a horrified expression on his ashen face.

"Good Lord!" he gasped "How many, Kildare?"

"Take it easy," Kildare advised. "There's nothing you can do about it now. It was an accident; everyone in this room knows that. I've let Scotland Yard think that Wu Fang was behind it all, so I don't think they're blaming you—not yet. You know the village of Glenderm, of course?"

"Yes," Kent said tensely.

Kildare shook his head slowly. "There isn't a living soul left in the village," he said. "Three hundred ninety-six, by actual count, all dead and every body turned green. Your death machine must have some strange action on the skin."

Kent breathed a short, choked prayer and slumped back in his seat, head buried in his hands. He remained that way for some time before he finally looked up. His face was haggard and drawn.

"Mr. Kildare," he pleaded, "isn't there something I can do, something to right this awful wrong that I have done? I'd do anything!"

Kildare walked over to the Britisher and laid a gentle hand on his shoulder.

"There's nothing you can do now," he said. "But there is something else very important. You know about Wu Fang now, and you must keep your machine guarded from that yellow devil. That affair at Glenderm is a terrible tragedy, I will admit, but the results will be worse if Wu Fang gets possession of your death machine or learns the secret of its construction.

"From what I've seen of the force of your invention, he would only have to sweep it over London a few times, like the beam of a beacon, and all the millions of people there would be killed instantly. You understand now why we are here."

"But what can we do?" Kent pleaded. "Should I take my machine to the government? I could turn it over to Scotland Yard and—"

Kildare shook his head firmly.

"No," he said, "that's why I made a special point of not letting Scotland Yard know about your causing the deaths in Glenderm. They would arrest you at least for manslaughter, if not for murder. By tomorrow morning all London, including Wu Fang and his agents, would know that you and your death machine were reposing on the Thames embankment at Scotland Yard headquarters. I doubt if Scotland Yard with all their facilities could prevent Wu Fang from getting hold of that machine and possibly you, too, so he could torture you until he learned the secret of its development. Did anyone besides the Trasks know of your presence here?"

"No," Kent said. "I'm sure we weren't noticed."

"In that case," Kildare said, "perhaps you and your secret are safe for the present."

The government man yawned; the comforting heat of the fire after being out in the cold rain was telling on him.

"I think," Kildare suggested, "that Jerry and I can both stand some sleep. We haven't closed our eyes for nearly forty-eight hours."

Kent was pacing up and down the floor now, clasping and unclasping his hands behind him.

"When I think that I'm to blame for—" he began.

"You've got to forget that part of it," Kildare interrupted him. "All of us here know that it was an accident. But keeping it out of Wu Fang's hands is much more important."

"Bing and I will stand on guard while you two gentlemen sleep," Kent suggested. "I know I wouldn't be able to sleep the rest of the night anyway. You will find plenty of bedrooms upstairs. Bing will show you the way."

But Kildare shook his head.

"No, thanks," he said. "This will be good enough. Just turn off the lights. This chair feels pretty comfortable to me. How about you, Jerry?"

"I'm pretty sleepy," Hazard confessed. "I'll try to get in a few winks, if I can."

Kent turned toward the stairs. Then he stopped.

"I think," he said, "if you don't mind, Mr. Kildare, I would like to show you my invention."

"Very well," Kildare agreed, rising.

HAZARD FOLLOWED them out into a back room that had apparently been used as a den. Trophies were hung about the walls, and a work bench had been built along one side of the room.

But the thing that interested Hazard most was the queer apparatus sitting in the center of the long table. It reminded him of a combination of an overgrown fire nozzle, a certain type of vacuum cleaner and an object that resembled a tea kettle. One end of it was open; from the other, closed end there were several wires leading to plugs on the wall. At the bottom of the rear part was a pistol grip and trigger.

"I want you to know about this," Kent repeated. "I'll try to explain it as briefly as possible. This ray machine is made so that a person can carry it about, on the field of battle, for instance. So long as the electric wires leading to the rear of it are not broken, it will continue to function as often as the trigger is pulled."

"There's no danger of its backfiring, is there?" Kildare asked.

"No," Kent answered, "it's carefully shielded at the back. All you have to do is point it at whatever you want to kill and pull the trigger." His face went white again.

"And believe me," he went on, "I didn't know it had such terrific force that it would carry for four miles or more and kill a whole village of people."

"Not only that," Kildare said, "but we saw the path of destruction that it wrought across the heather. It's the most powerful thing I have ever heard of. A country possessing a war device like that could rule the world, if it chose."

"Yes," Kent nodded. He set the machine down again. "But I almost wish that I hadn't developed it. However, I'll try to explain the working of it. My first experiment, which proved only partly successful, was a special adapter for an X-ray machine. But, as you know, that failed because it didn't have sufficient range.

"This is, as you can see, quite unlike an X-ray machine. It might best be described as a radio beam, but it isn't entirely that. It has an action upon the atmosphere that I myself can't fully describe. How it turns the skin green is quite beyond me, as yet."

"But look here," Kildare asked, "isn't there some way that a living body could be protected from it?"

"If there is, I haven't discovered it," Kent answered.

"But you said there's no danger of its backfiring," Kildare insisted.

"That's perfectly true," the inventor agreed.

"Then doesn't that mean that it's shielded at the back with some special metal such as the lead they use with X-ray machines?"

"No," Kent told him. "This resembles a directional radio beam. The ray or beam of death travels only from the opening, and unless you are directly in its path, you won't be affected by it. You could mow down a whole army by simply sweeping it in front of you."

He turned his back on the machine, and Hazard saw him shudder.

"Let's get out of here," he suggested. "I don't want to think about it anymore tonight."

Kildare laid his hand on Kent's shoulder and led him out of the room. At the door he turned, and Hazard saw that he was looking at the windows. The government man went back, made sure they were locked, drew the shades down, and turned off the light. Then he went out and closed the door.

Hazard dropped into the chair that he had occupied. Lightning flashed and thunder boomed outside, but within the fire crackled cheerily in the great open fireplace. Slumber stole quietly up on Hazard, and he slept.

When he first awoke, Hazard thought that it was the thunder that had brought him back to consciousness. But he knew that that wasn't all. Kildare was on his feet, gun in hand. Outside, the rain poured down in torrents and the lightning was so incessant that for a moment he thought it was daylight.

Suddenly, the newspaperman's eyes bulged from his head. They were riveted through one of the windows on a face—the ghastly, gleaming yellow face of a Chinaman.

The lightning showed him clearly, but Hazard realized that Kildare was looking at the next window!

Blam!

Hazard's gaze switched as Kildare's automatic barked out in the great firelit room. There had been a yellow face at that next window too, but it had vanished with the shattering of glass.

With a bellowing roar of anger, Bing O'Flynn was leaping for the front door.

"Stop!" Kildare yelled. "Don't go out—"

The last word that he was about to utter didn't come. It was choked off by a sound that seemed to come from far out on the moor. A crash of thunder split the air, and again the night was lighted with a weird, unnatural light. The cry came again. This time it sounded even farther away, but it was more audible.

"Kent! Kent! Don't—"

The words ended in a piercing scream of terror and torment.

CHAPTER 11
THE DRAGON'S CLAWS

KILDARE LEAPED for the door. The cry from out on the moor had seemed to change his mind completely

127

about going out into the night. He snapped an order to Bing as he jerked the door open.

"Stand here and don't let any living thing cross the threshold. Come on, Jerry."

Hazard, like Kildare, was clad only in his bathrobe and slippers, but nevertheless he snatched up another flashlight and his automatic and dashed after the government man.

Bam!

A flash of lightning, immediately accompanied by a terrific clap of thunder, zigzagged across the moors. Something moved beside them—something that glistened in the lightning flashes. A half-naked Malayan was leaping from the cover of a tree straight for Kildare, a knife in his upraised hand. The number one government man saw him coming, and without slowing his pace in the least, he swung his gun around.

Blam!

A big .45 slug stopped the attacking brown man in midair, and he dropped to the ground. Then they were tearing on through the darkness, charging through the gate, out into the open wastes.

"Confound it," Kildare mumbled, "I wish I could be sure of the distance that cry came from."

Something loomed ahead in the road, and Hazard saw that it was a car. A big, expensive phaeton, which he recognized at once as Trask's Rolls.

Kildare shot the beam of his light into the driver's seat on the right hand side. There was a body slumped over the wheel!

It was Trask, and his head was bare and covered with the matted blood that still oozed from his crushed skull.

"Quick, Jerry!" Kildare cried, as he climbed into the car. "I was afraid of this when I heard that cry. Help me get him over."

Together they dragged Trask's limp body to the other side of the seat. The motor was still running, but the lights were switched off.

"Get in behind that wheel," Kildare ordered, "and drive like the devil right through the gate and back to the lodge."

Hazard leaped in even as Kildare spoke and clutched the wheel that was wet with rain and slimy with blood. He shot the car into gear, stepped on the accelerator, and the Rolls leaped forward.

Kildare was fumbling about the dashboard. And the headlights shone down the road ahead of them, picking out the fence and narrow gate. Hazard tore through the opening at forty miles an hour. His right foot tramped on the brake pedal, and they slowed to a stop before the lodge.

Kildare had Trask's body slung over his shoulder as they charged across the veranda to the front door.

"Open up!" the government man shouted. "It's Kildare."

Then Hazard saw him tense—saw his flashlight probe the darkness. No sound came from inside. Hazard banged frantically on the door.

"Open up!" he shouted. "We're back!"

Crack!

An automatic barked somewhere in the living room, and a

cry of horror rent the air. Then the bolt slid back, and Kent peered out at them through a crack in the door.

Kildare and Hazard went in, the door slammed shut, and the bolt slid back into place. All three of them were staring down at the limp form on the floor.

Kent was down on his knees, crying, "Bing! Bing! Look at me. Are you hurt?"

Kildare rolled Trask's body off his shoulder and lowered it gently to the floor. There was still another form there—a squat, ugly Chinaman was still twitching in the last throes of death, a victim of Kent's automatic.

Hazard yelled as he saw something scurry across the floor toward Kildare. It looked like a rat dragging its tail, and the government man whirled and leaped into the air.

Bam!

He missed the little beast and sprang back as it lunged for him. Hazard's gun jerked up.

Blam!

The automatic went off with a deafening roar as the bullet traveled straight to its mark. The deadly creature was nothing but a bloody splotch of flesh on the rug.

"**BACK TO** the den!" Kildare shouted, springing for the door. "Come on, Kent, you can't do anything for Bing. He's past that stage now, poor devil."

Kildare darted back suddenly as the door swung open, ducked as something whistled through the air.

Crash!

His gun exploded in another thunderous roar. A figure came

plunging out of the den with lightning speed, and under his arm he carried the machine of death.

Hazard had turned and was trying to take aim, but the savage, brown-skinned Malayan was coming so fast and weaving so rapidly from side to side that he couldn't be sure of his mark. He pulled the trigger twice, but both shots missed.

Then from somewhere behind him, he saw Kent spring forward like a wildcat. He had no gun in his hand, but his fists were doubled. One shot out like a battering ram, and there was a short, sharp smack as bones snapped.

The half-naked brown devil's head snapped back, his knees buckling. As he fell, Kent snatched the death machine from his grasp. Just to make sure the Malayan was finished, Kildare let his gun bellow at the savage.

"All right," he said, "there may be more in here. At last we've got these devils where we want them. I only hope Wu Fang is either in here or out in the night. Hazard, get behind Kent with me."

As he spoke, he leaped behind the fighting inventor.

"Now," Kildare said through his clenched teeth, "turn on that death machine. Aim it so that it covers everything around this house. Turn it slowly. Point it upstairs. We'll show Wu Fang how this machine actually works. For once, we'll use him and his agents as human guinea pigs. OK, let her go."

With terrifying abruptness, the lights went out just at that instant, plunging the three men into utter darkness.

"The lights are gone!" Kent cried. "I'm holding down the

trigger and the switch is open, but there's no juice coming through."

Another roar of thunder crashed about them.

"Quick!" Kildare breathed. "Up the stairs! We'll be a little safer on the second floor. Is there a room up here with only one window?"

"Yes," Kent said. "Follow me and I'll show you the way."

At the bottom of the stairs, Kildare clutched the arms of both men.

"Wait," he whispered hoarsely. "Listen! Kent, you go first to show us the room. Crawl on your hands and knees."

"All right, if you say so," Kent said, "but I can't see—"

"Listen," Kildare hissed, "there may be somebody upstairs. If anyone sees you and you're down, that will give me a chance to shoot over you."

"I understand," Kent whispered.

"OK, let's go up now. Hazard and I will be right behind you."

As noiselessly as was possible they crept up the stairs. Hazard walked almost erect, so that he could shoot over the heads of Kildare and Kent if anything should appear to block their way.

They reached the upper hall, and Kent crawled on. He rose up enough to clutch the knob of a door. He opened it, and Hazard stared into the room as another weird flash of lightning illuminated the hall. So far as he could see, there was no one either in the corridor or the room that Kent was entering.

"It's quite all right," the inventor whispered. "There's no one in here."

Hazard gathered up the dragging wires and brought them

into the room. Kildare was waiting to close the door behind him.

"At least we're safe for a few minutes," the government man said after he had locked the door. "I wish this storm would keep up the rest of the night, but there isn't a chance. Our flashlights won't hold out for long, if we have to use them much."

Hazard fumbled around in the darkness and found a bed, some chairs, and a dresser. Kildare took a blanket from the bed and stuffed it into the crack under the door.

"You're sure," Kent asked hoarsely, "that that devil Wu Fang is behind all this?"

"Positive," Kildare nodded.

"But how," Kent demanded, "did he know we were here?"

"Very easily," Kildare told him. Apparently Trask realized what had killed the people in Glenderm and came up here to warn you, after he had evaded his Scotland Yard bodyguard. Wu Fang's agents picked up his trail and followed him."

"But I don't understand what happened to Bing," Kent said. "Good old Bing, he was certainly a loyal friend, if a man ever had one."

"Do you remember that little beast—that cross between a rat and a lizard—that was scurrying after me when Hazard shot him?" Kildare demanded.

"Yes, but—"

"That was it. One of Wu Fang's poisonous beasts."

Suddenly Kildare fell silent, and Hazard felt him clutch his arm. The gentle, ominous creak of a board came to them. It sounded again, this time closer to the door.

"They've found us," Kildare breathed.

As Kildare tiptoed over to the door, there came an almost imperceptible scraping sound from the base of it. Kildare drew Hazard to him and put his lips close to his ear.

"They're trying to push the blanket out of the crack under the door," he hissed. "Help me hold it."

HAZARD PUT his feet against the blanket and pushed. The sound ceased. Another board creaked.

Kent cried out, "Look!"

Hazard turned to stare.

Blam!

Immediately following that blast of Kent's automatic, there was a loud shattering of glass. A cry from outside the window came to them, and in the light of the electric storm Hazard saw a gleaming yellow form topple out of a tree directly opposite the window. Then all was darkness again.

"Kent, come here," Kildare whispered. Kent tiptoed over to the government man. "Stuff that hole in the window with bed clothing."

Hazard stared at the broken window, and even in the darkness, he was sure he had seen something move just outside the ledge. When the next flash of lightning came, it was gone.

Kent was busy at the window, stuffing up the hole. Every muscle in Hazard's body grew tense, and his eyes strained to pierce the darkness. From somewhere in that room over near the window, he heard a sound. Another crash of lightning drowned it out, but his blood was coursing through his veins like ice water, and his back felt as though clammy, phantom hands were caressing it.

Kildare made no pretense of remaining silent any longer. His next order came sharp and loud.

"Kent, turn on your light. There's something in this room! Must have come in through the break in the glass."

At the same time, Kildare's own flashlight went on, and in the beams of the two electric torches, Hazard saw a horrible little swiftly-moving object. He couldn't distinguish it clearly enough to tell what it was. It leaped from the side of the wall straight at Kent, who stood not more than a foot away.

Hazard and Kildare both chorused a warning: "Look out! On your neck! Kill it!"

Kent darted away, brushed savagely at his throat. A sudden cry of alarm and pain left his lips, and he stiffened. With a low groan, he toppled over on his face. His body bounced a little as it crashed to the floor, his muscles quivered, and he lay still.

Both Kildare and Hazard's lights were on. Kildare leaped away from the door.

"Stay where you are, Jerry," he cried. "Keep that blanket in the crack!"

Hazard blocked with his feet as much of the blanket as he could. He saw Kildare bend over the prostrate form of the inventor and examine his neck where the tiny messenger of death had struck.

"God!" he breathed. His light stayed on. "Stay where you are, Jerry," he repeated. "I've got to watch the window now."

"What was it?" Hazard gasped.

"It was some kind of a deadly insect, but Kent smeared it so badly when he tried to knock it off his neck that there isn't enough left to tell what it looked like."

Long minutes of awful suspense dragged by. Now and then sounds came to them between the claps of thunder, but they saw nothing more outside the window except the lashing tree branches.

Again and again Hazard prayed for morning to come and release them from this agony of waiting. The storm grew worse. The lightning was almost continuous and the thunder, so deafening that it shut them off from all other sounds.

Kildare's light went on and off, on and off, sweeping constantly about the room and outside the window, but the beam grew dimmer and dimmer.

There was no telling how many agents were in the house or outside. The place was probably alive with them. Undoubtedly Wu Fang himself was in direct command here on the very spot!

Kildare's light was barely discernible now. He shut it off finally and said, "Turn on your flash, Jerry."

HAZARD'S LIGHT blinked on and he saw Kildare bend down and pick up Kent's flashlight. He replaced his own worn-out batteries with those from the inventor's torch, which had been broken as it fell, and he switched his light on again.

"Tear a corner out of a sheet, Jerry, and stuff it in the keyhole. We must pack up every possible crack until dawn. We'll be all right if we can last until then."

Hazard plugged up the keyhole, and the minutes dragged

on and on. The storm was at its height, raging like a demon let loose.

The batteries in Kildare's flashlight were almost worn out again. It gave off only a faint, sickly yellow glow.

"OK, Jerry," the government man said at length, "I'll have to use your flashlight now."

Hazard handed it over. Again the room was lighted up. The storm seemed to abate somewhat, and the thunder claps occurred at greater intervals. The lightning flashes receded into the distance.

"We've got to have a light when we need it," Kildare said. "I'm going to turn this off now. We'll have to trust to our ears."

He switched off the electric torch, and they were immediately plunged into darkness. Hazard's ears strained to hear any noise from outside. A scraping sound, gentle, soft, and blood-chilling, came to him from somewhere around the edge of the door. He felt around the keyhole. Yes, that was still plugged with the bit of sheet.

"What's that?" Kildare demanded, flashing his light on.

Neither Hazard nor Kildare could see anything. The sound ceased, but Hazard was aware of a familiar odor, pungent and distinctly oriental. It was like the scent of incense coming from far off. It grew stronger.

"Kildare!" he gasped. "What is that smell?"

"I don't know," Kildare said. "It comes from this side of the room. Smells like incense. It's growing stronger—rapidly. Jerry, they're—"

Hazard's head was spinning. He heard the scuffling of

Kildare's feet, but he didn't seem to have the strength to turn around. With a great effort, Hazard managed to twist his head. He saw that Kildare had dropped over on the bed. He could just barely make him out in the darkness. Then he couldn't see anything. His brain was whirling in a bottomless abyss of darkness.

Hazard became conscious that he was being forced to breathe. Someone was talking to him, but the voice sounded far, far away. There was pressure on his face as though a mask covered his nose and mouth. He seemed to be drifting, floating. His chest was being forced up and down, up and down. Why didn't they leave him alone?

Someone else spoke, but he didn't understand the words, and he couldn't see who it was because it was too great an effort to raise his eyelids. Suddenly breathing came easier to him, and the pressure of that thing over his face was gone. Then that sea of darkness swallowed him up again.

He didn't know how long it was after that that he awoke. His head spun and his whole body still ached, but the pain was rapidly leaving him.

He heard someone say, "That's right, open your eyes."

He did open them, staring straight up. He was lying on a bed beside an open door. Dimly, he noticed that the door was splintered and the lock was broken. He didn't seem to have the strength to move his eyes and see who else was in the room, so he kept them focused on the door.

Strangely, there was a shadow there, the shadow of a girl.

CHAPTER 12
SHADOWS AT SEA

JERRY HAZARD was very weak and his brain wasn't working too clearly. At first, the shadow of that girl against the door had no significance to him. He didn't know where he was; perhaps this was a hospital and she was a nurse.

Slowly, certain things became clearer to him. It was daylight, and the sun was slanting in from some room beyond the girl. She must be standing in the doorway beside him, and in that manner the sun was casting her shadow against the door. He closed his eyes again wearily.

He heard footsteps and became aware that whoever had been in the room before was leaving now. Someone else came in, and he had a feeling that the person was bending over him. In spite of his semiconscious state, he almost jumped as a familiar voice came to him. No sweeter voice in the world could ever have reached his ears.

"Jerry."

It was soft and tender and vibrant with anxiety. Mohra was speaking to him.

Hazard forced his eyes open and stared silently. A girl was bending over him. But that wasn't Mohra. Her hair, so many things about her were different. He closed his eyes and opened them again.

"Jerry, darling, don't you know me?" she asked.

He tried to speak and managed to utter a few weak words. "Mohra—darling."

It was Mohra! Mohra's face, her lovely dark eyes. But the hair was different. What had happened to her? He breathed that question faintly.

The beautiful face above him smiled tenderly.

"Yes, I have changed, Jerry," she said, "but it was necessary."

"Wu Fang—" Hazard began.

"Yes, Jerry, I know." Mohra nodded. "But that was a mistake. You see, Mr. Kildare advised this change before you and he left for England. He didn't want you worried about the possibility of my being captured from the police guard that surrounded me."

Suddenly she bent down. Her face was against his; their lips were pressed close. After what seemed to Hazard all too brief a moment, Mohra lifted her head.

"Where's Kildare?" Hazard asked. "Is he all right?"

The girl nodded.

"Yes," she said. "He came out of it sooner than you did. I've been so terribly frightened, Jerry. They've been working on you for hours."

Hazard found strength to press her hand that was clasped in his.

"Everything is OK now, darling," he said.

A frightened look crossed her face as he said that.

"I'm afraid not, Jerry," she said, shaking her head. "Mr. Kildare told me about the death machine and what happened here."

"Yes," Hazard recalled. "I remember. He had the death apparatus in the room. I smelled incense, and then everything went hazy. Kildare fell over on the bed. I was trying to fight off a feeling of unconsciousness. We were in an upper room of the house."

"That's right," Mohra said. "And you are still in that same room."

"But I still can't see how you escaped from Wu Fang's agents in New York," Hazard argued. "The police cabled they hadn't seen you for four days."

"I started to tell you about it," Mohra said. "Mr. Kildare advised that I find a girl who could impersonate me. I succeeded in locating one that filled the part. She looked very much like me, except that she was much prettier. She was an actress who had been out of work for a long time."

"No one," Hazard assured her, "could be more beautiful than you, Mohra darling."

"You are prejudiced, Jerry," she said, smiling. Then she went on, "It was this girl that Wu Fang's agents captured. I am sure she will be perfectly safe, because they won't do anything to her until Wu Fang gets back. When he discovers the mistake, he will let her go."

"But where were you during the four days that the police couldn't find you?" Hazard asked.

Mohra laughed.

"You aren't very keen yet, are you?" she asked. "I got so terribly worried about you over here, Jerry. I wanted to be with you. I thought I might be able to help if I were here. You see, more than five days ago I escaped from my guards and took the first boat for England. I went directly to the Chief Inspector of Scotland Yard. Of course, I disguised myself when I left

New York. I made up my face differently, dressed in different clothes, and changed my hair.

"I knew one of his men here in London, who had taken a liking to me. I felt I could trust him. So I went to his house. He told me about you and Kildare being killed with the gas— about the theft of the death apparatus. Then he told me that I needn't have any fear of Wu Fang in England, because he and his agents were leaving for New York. I tried to find out which boat they were taking, but he wasn't sure."

"Good Lord!" Hazard breathed. "Wu Fang's agent told you that?"

Mohra nodded.

"YES," SHE said. "Don't forget that I've been an agent of Wu Fang myself. Strangely enough, his agents are human beings, in spite of some of the awful things they are forced to do."

Strength was returning rapidly to Hazard. He sat up with an effort.

"You know what that means, Mohra," he said. "It means that Wu Fang is headed for New York, for the greatest and richest city in the world. He has a machine that's so powerful that, from the top of the Times Square Building, he can wipe out every living inhabitant of Manhattan. We've got to get back to New York. We must send word to the naval cruisers to blast the boat that he's on and sink it."

"Mr. Kildare has already made plans for that," Mohra told him. "We are going to take the first boat out of Liverpool for New York."

The thin figure attacked viciously.

They heard footsteps coming down the hall, and a moment later the Chief Inspector looked in.

"I'm afraid there isn't any more time," he said. "How are you coming, Hazard?"

"He's recovering rapidly, thank you, Inspector," Mohra answered for him.

"Do you feel fit to travel?" the Inspector asked.

"Yes," Hazard nodded grimly, "of course."

Mohra put her arm about his shoulders and helped support

143

him as he slid his legs to the floor and stood up. He noticed now for the first time that someone, probably the Scotland Yard men, had dressed him in his clothing that had been hung up before the fire.

His legs wobbled unsteadily, but he could stand alone. He walked out into the hall, where the sunlight slanted through a window. Suddenly, he glanced at the Chief Inspector.

"How did you know we were here?" he asked.

"We searched for you most of last night," the Chief explained, smiling, "after you and Kildare vanished from Glenderm. This morning we found the path of destruction left by the death machine. We started to follow that when we were nearly run down by a car driven by your young lady friend here. After she told us what had happened, we got out here as quickly as possible."

The Chief Inspector shook his head.

"We thought you never would come out of it," he said. "Twice we decided to give you up but then"—he smiled at Mohra—"your very beautiful friend insisted that we keep on trying. You owe your life entirely to her, I assure you."

Downstairs, Scotland Yard men thronged the great living room of the Trask hunting lodge.

"You certainly are a sight for sore eyes," Kildare said, smiling. "I was greatly relieved when I heard you were coming around. You look like the happiest man in the world and I imagine"—he winked at the girl—"Mohra had something to do with it."

"Right," Hazard grinned, "but why didn't you tell me about another girl being substituted for her?"

Kildare shrugged.

"In the first place," he said, "I wasn't sure that she had made the substitution. It was merely a suggestion I made before we left New York. I had no way of knowing that she had acted upon it. Then, when that cablegram came from the police in New York, I was completely at sea. But remember, I said I was quite sure everything would work out all right. So far it has."

"Yes, so far," Hazard groaned. "What do we do now? Mohra says you have all the plans made."

Kildare nodded.

"Yes," he said, "come on. I'm going to try to get in touch with our fleet in Atlantic waters, so they can round up all ships that put out from Liverpool and make a complete search of them when they near New York. Then we're going to take the first boat that sails west."

He turned to Mohra and asked, "Would it be possible for you to learn from Wu Fang's agent in London what ship that yellow devil left on?"

"I'll try," she said, "when we get to Liverpool."

It was nearly dark when they reached the great British seaport. Hazard had eaten two good meals and was feeling quite fit again. Kildare seemed to show no ill effects from his narrow escape from death.

When they reached the docks, Mohra went into a phone booth. Hazard watched from outside, saw her talk a few minutes and then listen tensely. When she came out, her face was ashen white.

"He's gone!" she said in a low, hushed whisper.

"You mean the agent?" Kildare cut in.

The girl nodded.

"I talked to his servant," she said. "He said two men came to the house a little over two hours ago. They had some argument with his master, and he left with them, apparently very frightened. He hasn't returned."

Kildare's teeth clenched savagely.

"They've got him," he said.

"You mean they know what he told Mohra?" Hazard asked.

"Wu Fang or his agents have made a pretty good guess at it," Kildare said. "And they know, too, that they're going to be followed across the Atlantic."

They went at once on board the large freighter, the *Barton*, which supplied accommodations for twelve passengers. This new freighter was one of the fastest ships plying between Liverpool and New York.

The Chief Inspector of Scotland Yard and some of his men came on board to wish them success and offer them whatever help they might need.

"Thanks," Kildare said, "but I don't believe that we will need any further help, if our naval cruisers follow my directions carefully."

WITH A cheery farewell, the Chief Inspector left the ship and the lines were cast off. Tugs puffed and grunted as they moved the great freighter out into the harbor and started her on her way.

Kildare, Hazard, and Mohra were standing on deck, watching the lights of Liverpool fade away in the distance. The government man was smiling.

"I can well imagine," he said, "how relieved the Chief Inspector is to have Wu Fang and us out of the country." He turned and went below to the purser's office. "Come on, Jerry," he said, "I'd like to have you and Mohra go with me and find out some things—just in case."

"Just in case?" Hazard repeated.

"In case," Kildare smiled, "something should happen to me, I'd like to have you two know all the details so you can carry on.

"Look here, Kildare," Hazard said. "You aren't trying to scare me, are you? Wu Fang and his agents have already sailed."

"Yes, I know," Kildare affirmed. "We can count on that, but don't forget it's very possible that the yellow devil has left some of his agents watching to make sure that no one follows him."

Hazard and Mohra went with Kildare, and the newspaperman listened tensely to the questions that the government man asked the purser.

"What ships have sailed for New York out of Liverpool in the last twenty-four hours?" Kildare asked.

"The *Manchester* and the *Hereford,*" the purser replied.

"Will you describe these ships, please?"

The purser ran through a book of ship names and descriptions.

"The *Manchester,*" he said, "is a medium-sized passenger liner. It makes the trip to New York in six and one-half days. The *Hereford* is a heavy freighter. She generally makes it in nine or ten days, depending, of course, on the weather."

"You are sure that those are the only two ships that have left Liverpool for New York?"

"Yes," the purser said.

They went next to the captain's cabin. Captain Wilkins was a broad-shouldered, powerful man with leather-skinned face and neck that had been bronzed by years of exposure to the wind and weather. Kildare introduced himself and the others and explained their mission.

"So you're after the yellow devil, Wu Fang, are you?" the captain asked. "I've heard about him and the killings at Glenderm. A terrible thing, that!"

"Yes," Kildare admitted, "but not nearly so terrible as it will be if we don't capture him before he lands in New York. I believe you have accommodations for twelve passengers on this freighter, Captain. Is that correct?"

"Yes." The captain nodded. "But there are only ten aboard, however."

"And what is in the hold, in the way of cargo?"

The captain smiled.

"Tea," he said. "It's the first shipment of the new crop from India to head into New York. At least, we're hoping to make good enough time so that it will be the first. The first shipment, you know, always brings a high price in the tea market."

"I see," Kildare said. "And I believe you get a bonus for bringing in the first shipment."

"That's correct," the captain agreed.

"Is there any possibility of our overtaking the *Hereford* or the *Manchester* before we reach New York?" Kildare asked.

"We might be able to beat the *Hereford* in," the captain told him, "but there isn't much chance of our getting there before the *Manchester*. She's a fast little liner, and she's got a day's start on us."

"I have a very important wireless message to send," Kildare announced. "Will you come with me and read it? The wireless operator will probably want to ask your permission to send it."

The captain's eyes widened. "It must be quite important."

"It is—very. Will you lead the way?"

The captain took them to the wireless room stationed forward. Kildare's pencil moved swiftly across a blank radiogram page, and Hazard followed the message as he formed the words.

TO THE ADMIRAL IN CHARGE OF THE ATLANTIC FLEET:

DIRECT WAR SHIPS INTERCEPT FREIGHTER HEREFORD AND PASSENGER LINER MANCHESTER. CAPTAINS OF BOTH SHIPS TO STAND BY FOR INSPECTION. SEND THESE MESSAGES BEFORE YOU COME WITHIN FIVE MILES OF EITHER SHIP. WU FANG AND HIS AGENTS ON BOARD ONE OF THEM WITH MOST DANGEROUS DEATH MACHINE. IS EFFECTIVE FOR A DISTANCE OF AT LEAST FOUR OR FIVE MILES. ORDER CAPTAINS ON BOTH SHIPS TO CUT OFF ALL ELECTRIC POWER ON BOARD AS ELECTRICITY IS NECESSARY FOR USE OF THIS MACHINE. RADIO ME FREIGHTER BARTON WHEN CONTACT WITH THESE SHIPS

HAS BEEN MADE. WILL MAKE FURTHER SUGGES-
TIONS THEN.

SIGNED: VAL KILDARE,

U.S. GOVERNMENT AGENT.

Kildare tore the sheet from the pad and handed it to the captain.

"Perhaps you would like to read it before you sanction it," he suggested.

The captain's eyes widened as he scanned the message.

"By Jove," he said, "I had no idea it would be anything like this. Why, you're commanding the entire Atlantic Fleet to make special maneuvers!"

"That," said Kildare, "is to save every man, woman, and child in New York."

"Do you mean," the captain demanded, "that this yellow bounder has power to kill people at will with this machine he has stolen?"

Kildare shrugged.

"You heard what happened at Glenderm," he said. "No one was left alive in the entire village. And I happen to know definitely that Glenderm is four miles from the place where the machine was turned on."

"Good Lord!" the captain breathed. He turned quickly and handed the message to the operator. "You have my permission to send that message," he said, "and any other that Mr. Kildare may give you."

The captain accompanied them back to their cabins, which

were placed in a row on one side of the ship. Kildare's cabin was first, Hazard's next, and then Mohra's room.

THE GOVERNMENT man lowered his voice as he said, "About your crew, Captain, have you taken on any new men for this trip?"

"Not a one," the captain answered.

"You feel that you can trust all of them?"

"The shortest time that any of my crew has been on the *Barton*," the captain said, "is six months. I'd swear by every one of them."

"Good." Kildare nodded, satisfied. "Now about the passengers. There are seven besides us. I've seen only two or three of them."

"To tell you the truth," the captain admitted, "I haven't taken much note of the passengers as yet. But I dare say we'll all get a good look at each other at breakfast."

"No doubt," Kildare agreed. "And now I know you have your duties to perform, so I won't detain you any longer. Thank you for your assistance, Captain Wilkins."

Mohra, Hazard, and Kildare were all in need of sleep, so they turned in early. Next morning, they were the first to enter the little dining room of the freighter. One by one the seven other passengers began drifting in and took the places assigned them.

There were three women. One was obviously a school teacher; the other two, a mother and daughter who had been touring Europe. An elderly gentleman, distinctly British, entered and was ushered to his place. He was followed by a comfortable-looking man in the garb of a minister. The latter was rather stout, but his face was thin and wore a benign smile. Then an American businessman strode in, and last, a studious-looking young man, tall and thin almost to the point of emaciation.

Names meant little. It developed that the bespectacled young man was some sort of a professor. The clergyman was English, and his elderly compatriot addressed him as "Bishop." Hazard assumed that the two had known each other in England, Again, they might have chosen to sit next to each other because they were native countrymen.

During the three days that followed, one message came from the Atlantic Fleet. It was merely a confirmation that the admiral had received Kildare's message and was acting upon the government man's orders and turning about to head off the *Hereford* and the *Manchester*.

On the third evening, Hazard and Mohra were out on deck. The salty breeze was soft and gentle. Stars twinkled overhead but there was no moon. The decks of the freighter were large and ample, and the ten passengers were easily lost in the dark corners of the vessel. He and Mohra were standing at the rail of the afterdeck. He had his arm around her, holding her close as they watched the froth whipped up by the propellers.

For what seemed to Hazard the hundredth time on that voyage, he said, "Mohra, please change your mind. You know it would be so simple. The captain could—"

Quickly, Mohra laid two soft, caressing fingers on his lips.

"Please," she whispered. He felt her tremble a little. "It wouldn't be fair to you, Jerry," she said. "Not while Wu Fang is still alive. You would be in constant torment for fear that I would be taken away from you. Wait a little longer. I'm sure we'll get Wu Fang this time."

"I wouldn't be in any greater torment than I have been in the past, darling," Hazard argued, and caught her impulsively in his arms and crushed her close. He kissed her desperately.

Then all that was changed in one horrible split second. With almost superhuman force, Mohra pushed Hazard away from her and leaped back.

"Look out behind you!" she screamed.

CHAPTER 13
DEATH IN THE DEEP

SOMETHING SWISHED through the air—something that struck Hazard a crushing blow on the head and knocked him toward the rail. His head was spinning dizzily, but he wasn't out.

He heard Mohra scream again. He whirled and saw that the girl was fighting furiously with someone. He couldn't see anything clearly, but he lunged for that attacking figure. Like a flash, the man ran forward.

"Are you all right, Mohra?" Hazard cried.

"Yes," she gasped. "Get him!"

Hazard dashed on down the deck in the wake of the fleeing man. He caught a glimpse of his figure, saw that he was hunched over as he ran. It was hard to judge his height, but Hazard could tell that he was thin and gaunt.

As he raced around the corner of a rear cabin, Kildare's voice came from the other side of the deck.

"This way," Hazard yelled and dashed on. He raced the length of the freighter, but found nothing.

Kildare caught up with him, stopped and panted for breath. But Hazard didn't wait to answer questions. He whirled and dashed aft again to meet a figure running toward him. It was Mohra.

"Are you all right?" she gasped.

"Yes," Hazard said. "What happened? Did you see who it was?"

"No, it was dark and I couldn't get a good look at him. He tried to throw me overboard. He was very thin."

"Yes, that's right," Hazard agreed. "He was very thin, but that's all I could see."

"But your gun, Jerry," Kildare asked. "Didn't you have it with you?"

Hazard shook his head sheepishly.

"No," he admitted. "Heaven knows, I didn't think I would need it now. Everything has been so peaceful since we sailed three nights ago."

"It's late," Kildare announced abruptly. "Mohra, I think it would be best if you turned in."

"Yes," Hazard agreed, "I think that's the best thing you can do."

"Oh, I say," the Bishop cried, hurrying up. "Did I hear a scream or was it the sound of the wind? I was reading in my cabin and—"

"Oh, it was nothing," Kildare told the passenger and crew who had gathered about them. "One of the women passengers became a little frightened and nearly fell overboard, but she's all right now."

Hazard surveyed the passengers. They were all there and Hazard noted that the professor blinked nervously behind his thick glasses. He was the only one in the group who could possibly answer the description of the marauder. Hazard scrutinized him more closely. On the surface, he certainly seemed harmless enough. He couldn't believe that this was the man who had attacked them.

The passengers dispersed rather reluctantly, and Hazard and Kildare went back to Mohra's stateroom. They waited outside until she had locked her door. They tried it, to make sure.

"You keep watch," Kildare whispered to Hazard. "I'm going to look around and do a little investigating."

It seemed to Hazard that Mohra would surely be safe in her stateroom. The door was locked, and it was so heavy that it would be difficult to break it down. He walked around to the outside of the cabin. The entire tier of cabins, he knew, was built on a platform above the narrow deck.

The porthole was ample enough to admit a slim body such as the form of the attacker, but it was so high that Hazard could barely reach it with his fingertips.

The newspaperman went around into the corridor again, and stood there for some time close to Mohra's door. Finally, he couldn't resist the temptation to knock gently.

Mohra's soft voice answered instantly, "Yes, who is it?"

An evil face peered through the opening.

"It is I, Jerry," Hazard whispered. "Are you all right?"

"Yes," she said, "but I don't seem to be able to sleep. It's so terribly stuffy in here. Do you thing it would be all right if I opened the porthole?"

Hazard hesitated.

"Yes," he said after a moment, "I'm quite sure it'll be all right. I don't see how anyone could get up there and come in."

Kildare was coming back down the hall as he spoke.

"What is it?" the government man asked quickly.

Hazard explained, "Mohra wants to know if it would be all right if she opened the porthole."

To Hazard's astonishment, Kildare raised his voice so loud that it echoed down the corridor between the cabins.

"You're quite safe now, Mohra," he said. "Open the porthole if you wish. I'm sure we've got the marauder cornered somewhere in the hold. We'll have him captured before long."

Hazard and Kildare returned to their own rooms. Hazard lighted a cigarette and sat on the edge of his bunk. He took his automatic out and examined it to make sure it was ready.

With that in his pocket, he softly tiptoed out of his stateroom door again and closed it noiselessly. He walked toward the forward end of the corridor, where it was a little darker, and there found a chair.

Suddenly the appalling silence was broken by a cry coming from down the corridor, from Mohra's room. Hazard was on his feet instantly, racing down the hall, knocking on the door.

"Jerry! Jerry!" Mohra cried.

"I'm here, Mohra," he cried, pounding frantically. "What is it?"

He leaped back to the other side of the narrow passage and lunged, one shoulder hunched forward.

Blam!

He struck the door hard and with a crash that he knew could be heard from one end of the ship to the other. It burst open. It was pitch-dark inside.

"The porthole!" Mohra cried.

Hazard fumbled desperately for the switch, found it, snapped on the lights. But there was no one else in the room besides

Mohra and him. The girl, clad in a filmy silk garment, was huddled in one corner of the bunk.

"I woke up just in time to see someone coming in through the porthole," she explained, pointing to the opening. "When I cried out, he fled."

Hazard was out of the door like a shot, charging down the hall and out to the deck. There were sounds of scuffling and a muffled cry.

Then Kildare's voice rang out, "Jerry, come here! Up the ladder on top of the cabin."

A groping, moaning form lay on the roof at the government man's feet. It was the figure of a thin man.

"Recognize him?" the government man snapped.

Some of the crew came running up behind the captain as Hazard stared down at the thin man's face.

"The most peaceful passenger of all," Kildare said. "It's our friend, the bishop."

"The bishop!" Hazard cried. "But he is a stout man."

"He was," Kildare corrected, "but he's not now."

The man was getting up, and Kildare held his gun trained steadily on him.

"I hope you put up a fight," the government man said savagely, "because I'd be delighted to pull this trigger."

"Don't worry," the man said. "I won't. I know when I'm caught. I couldn't go through with it. I was out of a job and desperate. I had a friend who was an agent of Wu Fang, and I wanted to be one too. Wu Fang put me and my friend on the trail of young Trask. We followed him and got the others in."

"You were up at the hunting lodge?" Kildare demanded.

"Yes," the man choked. "Wu Fang told me that he might be followed. He was leaving me to watch the ships that sailed after his."

"And Wu Fang told you to meet him somewhere in New York, didn't he?" Kildare demanded.

The man shook his head stubbornly as he protested, "No, no, I can't tell."

"OK." Kildare shrugged. He nodded to the members of the crew. "Lock him up."

A steward was there with a yellow envelope in his hand.

"A radiogram for you, sir," he said.

There were only a few words in that message, but they told a horrible story.

CRUISER RALEIGH FIRST TO CONTACT MAN-CHESTER. RALEIGH FOUND LATER ADRIFT ALL HANDS ON BOARD DEAD. BODIES TURNED GREEN.

It was signed by the admiral of the fleet.

CHAPTER 14
CHINATOWN

"THE FOOLS!" Hazard cried. "They got too close to it."

"No," Kildare corrected, shaking his head. "You're wrong, Jerry. Wu Fang outwitted them. It was a very simple thing to do. The battle cruiser *Raleigh* probably sent a message to the *Manchester*, advising them that Wu Fang was on board and telling them to shut off the generators.

"They received a return radiogram, apparently from the captain of the *Manchester*, telling them that he had complied with their wishes. Then the *Raleigh*, in perfect good faith, steamed up to the *Manchester* to make a careful inspection and search for Wu Fang and his agents.

"When they got within four miles of the *Manchester*, every man on the *Raleigh* was suddenly struck dead."

Hazard and Mohra accompanied the government man to the wireless room.

WU FANG S.S. MANCHESTER

BE ADVISED THAT WE KNOW YOU ARE IN COMMAND OF THE SHIP. TAKE TO LIFEBOATS AT ONCE. THE ATLANTIC FLEET WILL BE FIRING UPON YOU ANY MINUTE.

SIGNED KILDARE

Kildare said, "If we can get Wu Fang in a lifeboat, he will have no electricity with which to operate the green death machine. It ought to be pretty easy for the ships of the fleet to pick him up then."

Kildare passed the radiogram over to the operator, who immediately began sputtering the message out across the Atlantic.

"Now let's go up to the passengers' cabins. I want to look into something there."

Kildare stopped before the door of the cabin that had been occupied by the alleged bishop. They followed Kildare into the cabin, watched him while he rummaged through two suitcases.

Then he raised the mattress. "This is more like it," he smiled, pulling out a strange-looking object from between the springs and the bed clothing. It looked not unlike a small ocean monster with short legs but no arms or head. He held it up and now, as he looked closer, Hazard could see that it was made of rubber and had a valve nozzle at the top.

Kildare wiped the nozzle off with his forefinger and put his lips to it. He began blowing, and as he did so the rubber contraption filled with air.

"What is it?" Mohra breathed curiously.

Kildare stopped blowing long enough to smile.

"It's a sort of balloon or rubber bladder that can be used for changing a person's figure," he said. "You remember the one we called the bishop who is now in the brig appeared to be quite a stout man. We didn't suspect the bishop of being the thin man who attacked you on the deck simply because he didn't have his stomach with him."

Kildare went out and they followed him once more. He tossed the false stomach into his room as he passed on the way to the brig.

He peered through the grating in the heavy door of the ship's jail.

"So you're the bishop?" he remarked.

"I'll never tell you a thing," the man snapped.

"Perhaps." Kildare smiled. "But I think you will change your mind. You know Wu Fang has methods of getting information out of people. You probably are familiar with some of them: torture, death, that sort of thing. I know some of those tricks, too."

The man's face went white.

"You wouldn't dare," he said huskily. "You're an officer of the law."

"Oh, wouldn't I?" Kildare countered.

They turned abruptly and went back down the corridor.

"This bishop," Kildare said, "is quite a wiry individual. There was a coil of rope on the cabin roof which he used to pull himself out of the porthole of his own stateroom. Then he crossed the roof and lowered himself into Mohra's room."

They entered the wireless cabin in time to see the operator typing rapidly as a message came over the wires.

"I think we're getting our answer," Kildare whispered. He read:

VAL KILDARE, FREIGHTER BARTON

THIS IS NO TIME FOR JOKING. I AM IN COM-
PLETE COMMAND OF S.S. MANCHESTER. ALL
PASSENGERS AND CREW ARE DEAD. LET THE
ATLANTIC FLEET FIRE AT WILL. THEY WILL HAVE
MOST DIFFICULT TIME HITTING US. YOU WILL
LEARN REASON LATER.

THE CASE OF THE GREEN DEATH

WU FANG

The following evening, the freighter *Barton* was only a few hundred miles off Long Island when Kildare stopped in at Hazard's room.

The government man carried two strange objects, one of which Hazard recognized instantly. He had a gas mask hanging around his neck, and under his arm he carried something large and bulky wrapped in a cabin blanket.

Hazard followed close behind as he made his way toward the brig. Kildare spoke to two stalwart members of the crew that they met on the way.

"Get a rope and come down to the brig," he said.

They nodded with polite "Yessirs" and then a moment later were following them.

Kildare took the key of the cell and handed it to one of the seamen.

"I want you to tie the prisoner securely to his cot," he ordered. "Then come out, and I'll do the rest."

THE SEAMEN performed their job quickly. Kildare strode in and closed the door behind him.

Calmly, Kildare fastened the gas mask about his face. A feeling of horror crept over Hazard as he watched the procedure through the bars of the door. Wu Fang tortured people to get information out of them, but he had never seen Kildare do it.

"You remember," Kildare said, "the gas by which you thought you had killed Hazard and me? Or perhaps you didn't have anything to do with it?"

"No, no, I didn't," the man cried.

The club descended towards Wu Fang's skull.

Kildare spoke again, his voice muffled by the mask he wore.

"But you were there and you know what it smells like. You are about to smell it again—Bishop."

Then before Hazard's gaping eyes, Kildare lowered the little tube until the opening was only a few inches away from the prisoner's face. He saw a vapor coming from the nozzle, hissing down into the man's face and almost covering him for a moment.

"Come on," Kildare snapped, "let's have that address in Chinatown. Where are you going to meet Wu Fang? I'm either

165

going to get it or kill you, and it's awful to die by this gas. I know!"

The prisoner writhed frantically, coughing and choking as he tried to get his face out of the vapor.

"No, no!" he screamed. An awful fit of coughing seized him, and he gagged as though he were going to choke to death. Then he managed to get out the words "All right, I'll tell. Stop! Don't kill me. I'll tell. It's—it's Forty-three Mott Street."

Again a fit of coughing seized him. Savagely, Kildare opened the nozzle, and the white vapor sprayed out again.

"All right," he snapped, "but that isn't all. Give me the rest of it. What's the secret sign? How do you get to Wu Fang?"

The man choked out, "I am to go there after dark, knock twice quickly and then once. When an attendant comes to the door, I will tell him my job is finished and he will lead me to Wu Fang."

"All right," Kildare snapped. "That will do." He came out and nodded to the two seamen. "Untie him and lock him up again," he ordered.

He led the newspaperman up the stairs to the captain's cabin. To Hazard's surprise, the captain was smiling.

"It was a lucky thing, Captain, you kept that old gas mask as a keepsake," Kildare said.

Next he unwrapped the blanket from around the great object he had held under his arm. Hazard gasped as he saw that it was the rubber, balloon-like false stomach that the government man had found in the fake bishop's stateroom.

Hazard knew that Kildare and the captain were both laughing at him.

Kildare laughed. "That wasn't gas. Remember how that gas that overcame us at the Trask hunting lodge smelled like incense?"

Hazard nodded.

"Well, the captain found some incense on board and I used that. There wasn't any gas."

"But the man choked as though he were going to die," Hazard insisted.

"So would you," Kildare chuckled, "if I poured some of this concentrated incense smoke in your face. Now let me check up and make sure that I heard correctly. What was the address, Jerry? I want you to remember that because"—his face sobered now—"you're built more like the fake bishop than I am. You see, Jerry, you're going to do the job as soon as we get to Chinatown."

CHAPTER 15
THE VENGEANCE OF WU FANG

THERE WAS one more message for Kildare before they reached New York. It was from the admiral of the fleet and read:

HAVE LOCATED S.S. MANCHESTER. SHE IS BEACHED ON SHORE OF LONG ISLAND. ALL PASSENGERS AND CREW DEAD. BODIES TURNED

GREEN. THREE LIFEBOATS MISSING. RESIDENTS
WITHIN FIVE-MILE RADIUS OF VESSEL ALSO
VICTIMS OF GREEN DEATH.

By special arrangement, one of the tugs that met the freighter *Barton* in the New York harbor carried Kildare, Hazard, and
Mohra to the Battery.

Hazard hesitated as he and Mohra were about to part.

"If there were any other way, darling," he said, "I would stay
with you."

There was a long, lingering kiss. Then they parted.

Four police officers took Mohra away in a prowl car, while
a dozen cops accompanied Hazard and Kildare to Chinatown
in sedans with the shades drawn.

"I think I've laid out the plans completely," Kildare said,
turning to the police. "You have another detachment on the
way here, haven't you?"

"Yes," the captain nodded. "I called headquarters and ordered
it. There will be more than a hundred men surrounding this
block."

"You'll need them," Kildare said. He turned to Hazard. "Now,
Jerry, this is how things should work. You go up to the door of
Forty-three Mott Street and knock, first twice and then once."

He thrust a small, round pasteboard box into Hazard's hand.

"There are a dozen pellets in there," he said. "There's phos-
phorus inside them. When you come to a junction of passages
or at every twenty paces, drop one of these capsules. That will
make a slight glow. We'll be following those lighted spots on
the floor."

"That's a mighty clever idea," Hazard said.

"OK, then," the government man said. "Go ahead and good luck. I'll be right behind you."

When he arrived at the address, Hazard knocked twice and then once on the door. A shuffling of feet came from inside the dark shop, and the door opened a crack.

Hazard tried to affect an English accent as he uttered the words, "My job is finished."

"You will come in, please," a Chinese voice breathed.

Hazard entered, and the door was closed behind him.

The Chinaman drew back a drape at the rear of the curio shop.

"This way, please," he said.

Hazard tossed a pellet to the floor, stepping on it as he slid through the curtain. There was a creak as a door opened. He saw now, by the dim light that burned in the back room, that there was a trapdoor in the floor. The yellow man raised it up, waited for Hazard to pass down first. That wasn't so good. If he dropped a capsule here, the Chinaman would see the glow. He decided to take the chance.

Ten feet down the passage, they came to a turn that led to the right. Hazard dropped another pellet and stepped on it. They went down another flight of stairs and came to a "Y" in the passage. Here the Chinaman led him to the left fork.

Hazard heard the sound of the Chinaman fumbling along the wall. The very side of the wall itself had opened up.

Hazard was thinking with lightning speed. A lever or a button had been touched in the darkness by the Chinaman.

Hazard moved quickly. In the scant light, he had seen a rock in the wall. It was loose and not much larger than a silver dollar. He took the capsule and moved it down, scraping hard on the wall to break it.

So this was the secret passage into Wu Fang's den! Would Kildare find that spot on the wall where he was pressing?

Here they were no longer in a corridor but in a small bare room. The floor, walls, and ceiling were all made of stone. The ponderous door of matched blocks turned back into the wall.

There was a real door at the far end of the room. The Chinaman knocked on the door and a little panel slid back. An ugly brown face peered through the two-inch opening. Hazard's guide spoke in a strange tongue. Then the door opened.

There were Chinese ornaments all about the place and a thick oriental rug on the floor. There was a table at the left covered with a silken drape.

Then the brown man stepped behind a hanging curtain, and for a moment, Hazard was left alone. He heard a soft, swishing sound from behind, and a voice, horribly familiar, spoke to him.

"Do not move," Wu Fang said.

Hazard spun around. A yellow beast of a man darted back away from him with his automatic in his hand.

Beside him, not four feet away, Wu Fang stood, a cruel smile on his thin lips.

The room was suddenly filled with agents of the yellow devil, half-naked brown men and powerful Orientals. Hazard's arms were pinned behind him. Wu Fang was before him, talking and chuckling.

"I WILL admit," he said, "that this is quite a surprise. However, I have made plans for just such a move on the part of you and Mr. Kildare. I am expecting someone else here at any moment."

Hazard gulped. What did the yellow fiend mean? Who was he bringing here? Mohra? His first thought leaped to her, but he dared not utter her name.

Hazard tried his best to put up a bold front.

"You have come to the end of your rope, Wu Fang," he said.

Wu Fang laughed in high glee.

"You are not in a very suitable position, Mr. Hazard," he observed, "to tell me that."

There was a stir behind the drape at Hazard's left. It moved aside, and a man was dragged in. He was naked except for a loin cloth wound about his middle.

Wu Fang turned his back on Hazard and addressed the newcomer.

"I thought until a week ago that you were a loyal agent," he said, "but I have information that leads me to believe otherwise. I brought you here from England to keep you alive until the beautiful young lady to whom you gave information could be brought face to face with you. I want her to see how you will die for betraying me to her."

Two white men—stout, husky, neatly dressed fellows—were dragging Mohra in. They flung her unconscious form down to the floor.

Everything reeled about Hazard. He knew only two things. Mohra was there and he was struggling like mad.

Hazard stopped his frantic struggling to hurl threats at Wu

Fang. He didn't know what he was saying—didn't realize—didn't care! Then he stopped short, panting. Mohra wasn't dead! Her eyes were open and she was staring up in horror at Wu Fang.

Mohra turned her head to glance at the agent who had betrayed Wu Fang in London. Then her panic-stricken eyes fell upon Hazard's face.

"Jerry! Jerry!" she gasped.

Wu Fang whirled around to the table that was covered with the silken cloth. His long-nailed fingers clutched the cover, snatched it away, and his hideous laughter rang out again.

All of Hazard's attention was suddenly turned upon the contents of that table. It was the green-death machine!

Wu Fang snatched up the nozzle and spun around. His fingers were on the switch. Mohra screamed, tried to sit up once more. The yellow devil's fingers were pressing the button.

There was a scream from the former British agent, who stood naked before the death machine. He was slumping and his body was turning a ghastly green.

Suddenly, other cries rent the air. A drape moved behind Wu Fang on the side of the room through which Hazard had entered, and a figure came charging through, holding a club in his upraised hand. It was Val Kildare!

Hazard heard a loud swish as the club descended toward Wu Fang's skull, but the yellow devil shifted like lightning to the side. Then the place was filled with blue-uniformed cops. New York's finest were on the job. They shut out Hazard's vision so he couldn't see what was going on in front of him.

Suddenly, the lights went out and they were plunged into

total darkness. Screams and shots rent the dank air. A flashlight blinked on, dimly illuminating the place.

Mohra was struggling with the ropes that bound Hazard.

"Jerry, are you all right?" she asked in a voice that was vibrant with desperation and anxiety.

"Yes, I'm all right," he cried. "Are you?"

"Yes. I'm trying to untie you."

Then in the light of an electric torch, they were being led out of the place and rushed off in a car to Kildare's apartment.

A little while later, the government man came in. He smiled a little wearily, lighted one of his long cigars with maddening calm.

"For heaven's sake," Hazard exploded. "What's happened? Don't keep us in suspense. What about the death machine and Wu Fang?"

Kildare smiled.

"The machine," he said, "is smashed into a thousand pieces, and its secret died with the inventor. We didn't dare save any part of it; it's too dangerous. As for Wu Fang, he's still down there. I have an idea that one of his agents turned off the lights and dragged him out before we could catch him. But I don't think he'll get away this time. There are thousands of cops surrounding Chinatown. Every corner and crevice is going to be thoroughly searched."

The government man walked over to the window and stood there, looking out for a moment.

"We'll probably hear any minute that the yellow devil has either been captured or killed," he finished.

Hazard caught Mohra in his arms.

"Do you hear that, darling?" he asked. "Wu Fang can't escape this time. They're going to get him. Remember, you promised that when Wu Fang was dead—"

"Yes," she said softly. "I'm waiting to hear."

Then their lips met, and Kildare, without turning from the window, observed with a chuckle, "I think it's clearing. You two ought to be able to see the new moon before long."

POPULAR PUBLICATIONS
HERO PULPS

LOOK FOR MORE SOON!

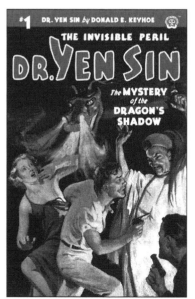

Made in the USA
San Bernardino, CA
25 July 2017